INSTRUCTIONS FOR A FUNERAL

STORIES

DAVID MEANS

FABER & FABER

First published in the UK in 2019 by
Faber & Faber Ltd,
Bloomsbury House, 74–77 Great Russell Street,
London WC1B 3DA

First published in the USA in 2019 by
Farrar, Straus and Giroux
175 Varick Street, New York 10014

Printed and bound in the UK by CPI Group (UK) Ltd, Croydon CR0 4YY

Grateful acknowledgment is made to the following publications, in which these stories originally appeared, in slightly different form: *The New Yorker* ("El Morro," "The Tree Line, Kansas, 1934," and "Two Ruminations on a Homeless Brother"), *Harper's Magazine* ("Fistfight, Sacramento, August 1950" and "The Mighty Shannon"), *The Paris Review* ("The Chair"), *Oxford American* ("Confessions" and "Fatherhood: Three"), *VICE* ("The Terminal Artist" and "Instructions for a Funeral"), *Zoetrope* ("Farewell, My Brother," "The Butler's Lament," and "The Ice Committee"), *BOMB* ("Carver & Cobain"), *The Best American Short Stories 2013* ("The Chair"), *Pushcart Prize XXXIX* ("The Ice Committee"), and *George Condo: Mental States* ("The Butler's Lament").

A CIP record for this book is
available from the British Library

ISBN 978-0-571-33095-9

1   3   5   7   9   10   8   6   4   2

The author would like to thank Genève Patterson-Means
for her enduring support and love.

INSTRUCTIONS
FOR A FUNERAL

ALSO BY DAVID MEANS

Hystopia

The Spot

The Secret Goldfish

Assorted Fire Events

A Quick Kiss of Redemption

To Jonathan Franzen and Kathryn Chetkovich

To refine, to clarify, to intensify that eternal moment in which we alone live there is but a single force—the imagination.

—William Carlos Williams, *Spring and All*

CONTENTS

INSTRUCTIONS
FOR A FUNERAL

CONFESSIONS

THE WORK

I've been writing stories for thirty years now, many published, others not published but trashed, put to bed, dead in the water, so to speak; lost to me, to eternity, or whatever. There's simply no way to distill or describe what's in the stories, except to say I attempt, to say the least, to respect whatever each story seems to want—not only to want to be, but to say in its own way—each one, as far as I can see, an expression of a particular ax I must grind, particular souls in particular situations, and in some cases a voice that needs to say what it says or else (and I feel this, really, I do) it'll be lost forever to the void, the same place where most stories go, forever; the real stories of men and women who lived lives—quiet desperation!—and then died, gone forever into eternity, so to speak. It's a gut feeling, a need to reveal something and to pin it down forever, and it involves a lot of revision, fixing mistakes and covering tracks and making amends with the material itself, so that what comes out in the vision is clarified, sharpened, and made clear—to me at least, if not to the reader, who might or might not get what I want, and most certainly will get something I didn't know they'd get. That's the best part, knowing that you'll be betrayed by the reader, so to speak, no matter what you do, no matter what kind of care you take with the work: you go into the senseless vision of the vision and then you revise it into something as clear as possible and leave it at that, striking out by letting it go out, and if it's taken into the arms of print, so much the better, you say to yourself, while also feeling, at the same time, a sense that it might not be for the better: in other words it might fail you, and the reader, and pin your name in the air overhead, above the story for a few days, or years, or a hundred or more, only to find its way into the void of eternity, so to speak, lost and gone. You're aware— at least I am—that eternity will devour everything in its own time, and that whatever mark is left will be gone, because that awareness is essential to the work: a sense of catching some slice of time itself, making it stand at attention, and still. If not for the sake of a reader—somewhere in the future—then for your own sake, for a moment, at the desk on a hot summer afternoon, or wintry cold day (it *does* matter) while also know- ing it doesn't matter one iota, really, because the persistent nature of time in relation to life is one of consumption, of time consuming life to bone, ash, dust to dust and all of that, so to speak, but for one eternal moment, the work might, or might not, live in the fire of neurons, brain to brain, in the soft silence again of time, and then fade, or, rather, fall, into nothing.

VIOLENCE

You'd better know what it is, really know, inside your flesh, before you venture in there, and if you're making a story around some violent act just because that's the central concern, or the thing your imagination latches on to, or you want to find a bridge between your inner life and the culture—which of course is most certainly violent—then you're doomed, because you're trivializing the violence by turning it into a useful tool, and no matter what, the violence you create will supersede the situation, the human situation; and though the human situation might be irredeemably bleak in the story, in life it is always surrounded by landscape, or people, who, seemingly against their will, provide symbolic grace, something beyond the horror of the violence itself, I think, at least right now, considering my father, who taught me to see the way I see, for good or bad, and who, even when facing violence himself, in one form or another, trusted in reality. In other words you'd better know what you're doing, I tell myself. You'd better have a wider worldview and a sense of cosmic justice at hand. Who am I to say? Just writing about it I feel myself taking a grand stance, but the fact that I'm writing in the confessional mode, here, isn't because of shame, not anymore, but out of a sense of humility and a respect for the truth, not wanting to betray the truth. It isn't a matter, really, of being afraid to expose my family—my sisters, my mother, my now-dead father—but because to find a way into the truth in fiction I can do so only by protecting them, working around them, giving respect to the complexity of a reality that served up to them a certain kind of violence, vague as that might sound—and it does, it really does, as if I'm skirting the intensity of seeing my sister devoured by her illness, living in squalor, in agony, walking alone on a wintry day, through the windblown snow up Westnedge Hill, wearing my trilby hat, the one I had been madly searching for back at the house, one day, years ago.

LOSS

To reckon with loss is to reckon with what hasn't been lost, I sometimes think, gazing out the train window, examining the river, trying to find a way into imagining the story that might come out of it someday, watching the small nubby hills give way to Bear Mountain, the tunnel, the bridge overhead slipping behind as the tracks swing past West Point, across the water, the stately hard limestone buildings—no sign of warfare or drill marching. Back when my father was dying I said again and again, at his bedside, How are you feeling? What are you thinking? I wanted him to come to me with some deep thought, some wide, arm-spreading notion of the way he felt in relation to his past, some keyed-in notion of how his anguish touched other moments in his life. I wanted a dramatic statement that reached back—the lake dock, a moment in the sun with his brothers, lying against the stony Canadian beach, chest heaving after a swim, as he remembered it in relation to the hospital setting; some weirdly twisted and yet clear-cut statement that I could carry and chew and eventually use in a story. Instead, his statements were blunt, sharp, and rudimentarily inward, always about his body as it felt at that particular moment, pinpointing pain—arms, legs, feet, feet, feet—or a need—to piss, to shit, to loosen the blood pressure cuff. He is consumed in the vortex of the moment, I thought, I think, and that was that; his eyes told the story—as he leaned forward to get out of bed, refusing my help, his arms quivering gently, the skin opaque and thin, widening to the bloom of bruise where the IV slipped in— that his only concern at the moment was twisted into the anguish, *ribboned* in—as I thought of it, and still think—as if all of time were nullified by a single, simple task; as if my only obligation at that juncture was to refuse my own need for something more, as I had refused it in the past, year by year. He was a man stoic and blunt. He had come from the cold, unyielding prairie and was returning to it, his eyes said. I will be gone and all this will be gone and you will not be seen by me as I don't see you now, his eyes said. In the hall, I wept as quietly as I could and walked down to the lounge where, through the floor-to-ceiling windows, the blue-black wintry dark tried and failed to provide an honest answer.

FISTFIGHT, SACRAMENTO, AUGUST 1950

The fight began in a tavern called the All Star, on the outskirts of Sacramento, when a young man named James Sutter leaned over and said, vaguely, as if to no one in particular, Man, do I fucking hate Okies, and a young man named Frankie Bergara responded by lifting a fist to his chin and nodding his head slightly in the direction of the door, a gesture that said: Step outside! Sutter, in turn, reached up with his closed fist and gently touched a knuckle to his own chin. (The girls loved Sutter's chin, square and dimpled in the center. That much was for sure. The girls loved the authority of his movement, the way he stepped in his expensive boots. They admired his ease, the way his tailored cowpoke gear rested on his strong shoulders.) Bergara was short and husky, with thick, rounded shoulders, a shock of curly hair, and a broad face weathered from the sun. He moved with a slight hobble, as if his legs bowed around an imaginary saddle. His heavy arms swayed loosely at his sides as he walked down the back hallway through the smell of sawdust and urinal cakes. Kicking the back door open, aware of his cheap knock-off boots, inherited from his big brother, he felt—stepping into the warm air—a deeper inheritance that came from countless barn-loft fights with Cal, fighting until the two of them began to laugh and then his brother released his grasp, stood over him, gave him tips on technique, always ending by saying, "Don't forget, kid. If you can't get him honest, get him with some kind of sucker, because to lose a fight is to lose a fight, and to win one is to win one."

Meanwhile, Sutter went out through the front door, gathering a few spectators, mostly friends, strutting lightly with anticipation. He had been trained to fight by the family handyman, Rodney—whip-thin, dressed in overalls—who would put down his wrench, or rake, or paintbrush to offer a few tips, saying, "Dip low with the shoulder and round yourself over the punch and get back as fast as you can, focusing your weight on the arch of your foot. As long as you're aware of your feet—even if you're not aware that you're aware—as long as you keep them in mind, you'll win." Rodney, who was taciturn and quiet as he moved about the house, fixing things, clipping the hedge, had fought Golden Gloves in Chicago before moving west. When he spoke about fighting his words had an oracular quality. In the few seconds it took Sutter to walk around the back of the building, where Bergara was standing alone beneath the single streetlamp, rolling his shoulders, in those few seconds he had a keen sense that it had been bad form to call Bergara an Okie. The Sutter line had Okie roots. His great-grandfather had come from Tulsa. But that truth—he felt this, rolling his own shoulders—was buried under recent good fortune. He was going to follow in his father's footsteps in the fall and attend Yale. Anyway, Bergara was mostly Basque, or something like that, a mixed blood that gave him curly hair, big shoulders, and a fireplug chest.

There were about fifteen kids behind Sutter, most of them from town. Behind Bergara, a few ranch kids stared at the ground, or out at the land behind the tavern. The town kids wore genuine silver belt buckles, plaid shirts with pearl snaps, and had hair barbered close to their clean necks. The ranch kids had faded jeans and T-shirts rolled tight around their biceps, and windblown hair. They watched as Sutter threw a few phantom punches and then stopped to take off his class ring, tucking it in his watch pocket. Bergara put his fists in position, scrutinizing Sutter as he reached and touched his collar and then ran his fingers through his thick hair before putting his own fists up. The touch of the collar was the habitual move of a kid who wore a tie most of the time. It seemed to be saying, *Punch me first, you two-bit dirt hopper, toss the first one at me and let's get this started so I can get home and take a nice, long, warm bath.*

The kids on Bergara's side had watched him fight enough times to know his tics, the way he retreated after landing a punch and shuffled a few seconds with his arms straight down and his chest pushed forward before heading back in. He'd taken much bigger men. Speed came cheap in these parts, but his ability to take his time, to fight carefully, seemed to come not only from the brutality of his life, from the chores he did on the ranch, lugging water lines, working the fences, and all that livestock shit, corralling and branding and shoving, but also from the patience he had learned standing in a field with a flag, waiting for the duster plane, staking out the horizon, aware of the surrounding grid of acreage. Then, with the bandana around his mouth and the flag raised, he guided the first sweep of pesticides, standing as far to the side as possible but close enough to go back out to guide the next release, the sound of the plane fading to silence until it circled around again. As they watched Bergara—in that split-second tension before he threw his first punch—they saw the weight fall back on his heels as his arm began a forward motion and then, suddenly, moved back again as he gave a warning to Sutter, to avoid making a sucker punch. Then he threw a hard jab to Sutter's solar plexus. It was a good, clean punch. Sutter saw it coming, but it still connected. (Some of the rich kids on Sutter's side had not seen the warning move, or the stepping back, and scored it as a sucker punch.)

Just before the jab, in the tension as Sutter stood with his hair fluffing in the breeze, it was possible, if you were looking carefully, to see that he was thinking about his place in the world in relation to how it might look to Bergara. Time lives retrospectively inside a fight. It doesn't slow down. It tightens so that one move locates a relation to the moves before it. The point of a fight like this was to reverse the flow of time, to reduce everything to an effect and cause, and in doing so to erase the everyday tedium of time. Everything that happened before the jab meant something. Everything after the jab gathered meaning in the moments before it was created.

You must never disregard your place in this world in relation to the way folks see you, Sutter's father liked to say. *We've had good luck along the way but it was only luck, and to think of it as some God-given truth puts you in a dangerous position. To think you're in his good graces is to throw yourself off-balance, and to be off-balance is to open yourself up to the whims of those who have a better footing in the truth*. (These words were usually spoken after dinner, with a damask of port glinting in candlelight.) *I've done some of my best speculating with a full-blown awareness that luck was the only thing involved, and not some sense that everything I have here*—his father said, sweeping his arm from one end of the dining room to the other—*came out of Providence, but more out of the way I've been able to corral my chances into a formable stampede.* And then his thoughts would begin to unravel because he was a man who theorized and speculated beyond his abilities and often found what at first seemed to be profound and weighty thoughts breaking apart into something lacy, gauzy.

Sutter held his arms up and kept his mind on his feet. The wind suddenly rose, bringing the smell of jasmine, dust, and gasoline. In his ringing ears, he could hear the faint, absentminded whistle Rodney made in the garage when he was working alone, concentrating on something—a saw cut, or getting a wrench into position, or when he was out trimming the box hedge along the back of the house. And he was hearing that sound as he unleashed the wild, flamboyant haymaker that had begun secretly, as he was stumbling, relieving the force of Bergara's punch back onto his heels, transferring energy as his shoulders rotated to his left while his arm, ambling in a wide arc, moved back to catch up with the rest of his torso (his fists tightening, fingers curled)—and then, in what looked to those watching to be one fluid movement, his arm moved on its own accord, landing his fist on the point of Bergara's chin, sending him sprawling back into the arms of his friends, who held him for a few seconds, saying, "Take his fucking head off, Bergara, do it for your brother."

The fight stayed inside the circle of light from the streetlamp. A daytime fight would have no such borders. A daytime fight would often move from the back of a bar all the way to the front; or into the field; or, in some cases, depending on those fighting, it would end with the blow of an implement, a scrap of lumber or a crowbar. Nighttime fights had the formality of the circle surrounded by night wind and the cool dark.

For a few seconds, as the two fighters stood and swayed, there was a silence that expressed a need for a larger narrative. It wasn't enough, the air said, to simply fight over the Okie comment. It wasn't enough to have one more Sacramento fistfight between a wealthy town boy and a ranch boy. The air begged for a deeper significance.

Then someone said, "Kick that silver fucking spoon out of his teeth, Bergara," and on Sutter's side, someone said, "Knock the clodhopper's jaw off, clean his yokel clock," while the girls remained silent—there were three or four of them—and pitted the elegant beauty of Sutter's dimples and clean jaw against the rough, blunt complexity of Bergara's face.

(With the exception of a young woman named Sarah Breeland, who worked the fountain at the five-and-dime store in town and had talked with Bergara once or twice, setting a milkshake in front of him, seeing in his eyes the sophisticated kindness that came from hard toil. Knowing, too, talking to him—he spoke carefully, his words barely audible in the din of the store, the cheep of canaries in the pet section, the popcorn machine popping—that he understood a certain type of quiet that came from living on the margins, not only of life but of the town itself, for she lived in a house not far from his ranch, tending her sisters while her mother went to the Sutters' home to clean. She had gone a number of times to the Sutter house to stand with her mother and watch as she worked the iron-press, the starchy steam puffing as she pushed the lever down and made tight creases while her nimble fingers lifted and readjusted.)

Sarah caught Bergara's eye as it swayed over Sutter's shoulder and gave him a slight smile and a nod, as if to indicate that a secret might pass between them.

Years later, she'd remember the way he had nodded back at her, once, quickly. She'd remember the taste of the dust in the air and the scent of juniper. She'd see the significance, the hugeness, of that single glance, and the luck of having arrived at the tavern, hearing the shouts out back, and for some reason—she liked to think it was her deep sense of pity, of wanting to be there to care for those who were beaten—walking around to watch. She liked to think she had been looking for Bergara, searching him out. But of course that wasn't true. He was just one more ranch boy in a line of many.

•

As Bergara lifted his shoulders and thought of his brother fighting in Korea, freezing his balls off, Sutter reached up to touch his collar again and then raked his fingers through his hair, smiling slightly before sending a quick jab to Bergara's shoulder (a true sucker punch) and then, in a flash, a cross that landed at the bottom of his jaw (a countersucker) and sent him stumbling to the left, staggering slightly, and then, closing in, two quick jabs to Bergara's face with his right and a hook with his left to the mouth again. When Bergara stood he looked startled and dazed. He spat a tooth to the side with an offhanded sideways motion.

Truth is, there was a deadlock of sorts at this point in the fight. Bergara with his hard past and his mean father (they all knew how his father was when he was drunk) and his toil in the fields and the way he had learned to fight to the end, one way or another, who had to win however he had to win, if not for the sake of his brother in Korea and the family's ill fortune then just because the word *Okie* still resonated. Against Sutter, who had all the good graces of the town's richest kid combined with an open-ended, all-knowing sense that he was destined to win not only at fighting but at life itself, to go off to Yale at the end of the summer and frolic in the east for a few years—picking up new habits but never forgetting home—and then come back for a job at his father's bank, taking the train through the forlorn Midwest, stopping at depots for fuel and water late at night, staring out the window at the quaint scenes: the stationmaster behind the window in the green shaded light, sorting waybills and bulletins as the train moved forward, passing through sleepy towns with houses squatting on the hillsides in the wee hours of night.

Justice didn't seem to be factoring into it at all. There was nothing at this point in time to indicate that the pain Bergara's family had endured over the years would in a single moment be sanctified and honored. There wasn't a sense of egalitarian, all-American fair play. None of that seemed to matter. The crowd simply felt the thrill of watching Bergara spit his tooth to the ground. The white, bony fragment in the dust. The glimmer of his spit. The blood on his face as he stood with his arms straight down, shoulders back, eyes glaring.

Weeks after the fight, those who knew Bergara would attempt to locate a relationship between the punches he threw next and the blow that would strike him a month later when a U.S. Army car came to deliver the telegram with the news of his brother's death. One more boy gunned down on a hillside in the Chinese counteroffensive. That kid's brother was in Korea and that put him into a better fighting spirit! He didn't know he was doing it, but he threw those punches in honor of his brother! He hit hard because he knew he'd get hit hard!

A punch lives and dies in a flash but continues on as a tactile memory, hovering between two souls: the way it felt for the puncher, unleashing it, and the way it felt for the person receiving it. Sutter was back on his heels, relishing his glory, destabilized, struggling to regain his posture, when Bergara charged, closing in quickly, jabbing at Sutter's chest—the follow-up coming instantly, a second punch that sent him sideways—Bergara had him in a clinch, and then, after that, an uncountable flurry, the arm moving forward and back, forward and back.

(As he received the punches, Sutter felt the shame of loss. Each punch established a home in some deeper, spongy part of his mind. Each punch shook a doubt loose in his brain, and before he could shove it back, another one came, and another.)

Nobody had taught Bergara how to throw a pivot blow (also known as the "rabbit" punch). He felt inventive as he pivoted and drew his arm back—in one quick fluid motion—and then rotated forward in a motion outlawed by professionals because it was deemed too mechanical, too precise, too blunt, too old-fashioned, too inelegantly elegant, and drawn too squarely in the air to fit in with the loopy, sweeping give-and-take of the sport. (He would see this punch after the fact, in a hazy retrospect, hardly remembering how it had played out until Sarah told him later, confessed softly, saying, I've never seen someone punch like that.)

Much later, he would try to justify the rage he had felt, the thoughtlessness that had overtaken him in those final moments—when the crowd, suddenly frightened, began pulling him away—by pinning it to Sarah's glance, her deep brown eyes, the way she had nodded at him over Sutter's shoulder.

Sutter called me an Okie. That's what started it all. I didn't mean to give him a concussion, or break his jaw. But like my

brother told me, the only good fight is one you win, and only win-
ning makes it a good fight. I'm sure that because your mother
worked for the Sutter family, and because he was the way he
was, he probably tried to make a move on you at one point or
another.

•

A few years later, in Arizona, sitting out on the patio with a
beer after working the day shift, watching Sarah lift the laundry to the line, a clothespin in her beautiful mouth, her thin
arms freckled, her windblown hair bleached blond, Bergara
thought about that fight, saw it filtered and bent through time,
beginning with the summer romance it had inspired, driving
in his truck on back roads, stopping to take the old horse blanket out of the trunk, spreading it across the warm hood, lying
back against the windshield to watch for shooting stars. The
fight was filtered through that night, a few weeks later, as they
lay hip to hip, hand in hand, and she began to talk—her voice
husky, deep, arriving out of the depths of her lovely neck, saying, Frankie, there's something I wanted to tell you, about
Sutter, and he said, Yeah, go on, and she said, You were kind
of right, about him making the moves on me when Mom was
working at his house.

He was putting into retrospect the sight he'd caught of her
in that slight lull of action, when the crowd grew quiet and
stood back and waited. Just a quick glance, nothing special
really. One more of those girls during a break in a fight, some
spectator in a skirt and bobby socks with a fresh young face
looking on with a lovely presence, lipstick bright and shiny
and perfect against pale skin, pleading with her eyes, seeming to make a judgmental statement, the eyes squinting for a
half second, as if trying to see into his own while saying: *It*

isn't enough to see this fight as simply tit for tat, one guy bait-
ing another into a rumble to pass time, to get a better sense of
who was who in the pecking order. It isn't enough to explain it
as a rite of passage, as something to break apart the brittle ten-
sion between the Sutters of the world—fluid with entitlement,
with fresh-laundered shirts, iron creases still visible—and
ranch kids with a history going back to the hop pickers (nothing worse than a fucking hop picker, his father liked to say)
and the migrant crews that came for free potatoes and shelter
and waited a few weeks until the hops were ripe and ready to
be picked, feeling at night the firm, hard pressure of the ladder
rungs under their feet, the lug of the bag strap pulling their
*shoulders. This has to be—*her face in the crowd said—*part of*
a wider story, and that story should include me, later, after-
ward, because we're gonna use it to find out that we love each
other, and this fight, this first meeting of sorts, will get us talk-
ing, sharing the secretive, soft give-and-take that will come
from learning that in spite of the fact that I dress well, and hold
myself with a comportment, at least as you saw me in a glance,
in the heat of the fight, with most of your mind on Sutter, and
the bearing of a rich girl, you'll come to learn that I'm really just
another poor girl on a scholarship to the Young Women's Acad-
*emy, an outsider as much as you are, so that years later—*right
now, Bergara thought, on the patio, me and this beer and my
own little house, not much but my own, and the baby on the
way—*you will remember this fight and look back at it remem-*
bering how we met up afterward and how I told you, as she
did, *saying, Momma was downstairs in the laundry room,*
ironing, and Sutter came up to me in the kitchen and then he
started grabbing at me, playing around, yeah, but grabbing
while I told him to stop it.

A few days after the fight she had tried to tell him about

Sutter. They were in the soda shop and she was again placing before him a tall chrome shaker of malted milkshake. Behind him the smell of popcorn and the cedar chips from the pet cages combined with the woody clomp of customers and the sharper sound of the men along the counter clicking their silverware to make her words inaudible. What did you say? he said. I'll tell you later, she said, and then she went down the counter to tend to another customer, holding her check pad up as she walked, attentive and sure. He watched her and shook his head and went back to his milkshake.

I felt a vindication, he was saying, out on the patio, leaning back in a rusty lawn chair, bringing the beer to his lips.

She was removing a handkerchief from her hair, pulling it down around her neck and fingering the knot. Beyond her—on the edge of Tucson—the sunlight burned against the foothills.

When I kicked the shit out of that Sutter fellow, I felt it then. It's as if I knew you'd tell me that story you told, he said. He took another sip and watched as she shook her head softly to the side and then smoothed her dress against her hips, thrusting her belly out, patting it gently with the flat of her hand, turning to give him a profile view as he sipped the beer.

Ah, forget it, he said, and he meant it. He wanted to bury that night in the past with the other painful moments: standing out in the field after the duster. The spray bitter and tarlike. The bandana tied to his mouth. Mending the fences with his fingers bleeding. Leaning into the crushing weight of stubborn livestock. His father's thick hands on the belt.

I was just thinking, he said, watching as she hung the bag with the pins on the line and walked over and settled down into the chair beside him. Suddenly they were simply two more married souls on the edge of a new development; two more sharing a moment together, relishing a sensation of glory, waiting for the first stars to appear.

Where'd you come up with a word like that? she said.

A word like what? he said, patting his own belly.

Vindication, she said, smiling. He loved the look on her face. He loved her face. He loved the down on her neck. Honey, that's a look that gets me through the day, he sometimes said. When I'm folding boxes, or loading a pallet onto a truck, I think of that look. When I'm punching the clock, that's the smile that gets the card into the slot.

Just came to me, as I was thinking things over, he said.

She turned and looked beyond the yard and they settled into the kind of silence they would, later in the marriage, take for granted. Now it created a tension, a paradoxical sense of needing to speak and stay silent at the same time. But later, after a move to Cleveland, they'd feel keenly that this kind of quiet was what love became when it hardened into history, one day after another passing behind them, because that shared sense of destiny that began that night, during the fight, would never leave. It was the secret, they both liked to believe, they had shared in that first glance: a boy looking up, his face sweat-sheened and tight, and a girl looking on, pursing her lips slightly in a way she had seen in older girls, that went beyond her mother working in the Sutter household, or his own misery at the time. It was the secret of their future destiny. That's what they liked to believe. That's what they continued to believe for the rest of their lives.

You weren't thinking about vindication when it was happening. He hit you hard, if I remember correctly, and then you hit him harder, and he hit you a little bit harder and you lost that tooth, and then you happened to be the one who hit him the hardest in the end, she said.

I fought dirty. Time's gonna be the final judge, but I fought dirty.

I love you anyway, she said.

And I love *you* anyway, he said, feeling the cool patio stones on his bare feet.

In Cleveland he'd claim: *I knew it right then. I knew your name and that your ma worked for Sutter's folks. That put the fuel in me and made me want to kill that bastard. I guess I'd even go so far as to say I knew exactly what you were thinking, somehow, and had it all figured out.*

Much later—maybe in Detroit, or their last year in Toledo—he'd remember it differently. He had looked at her and known intuitively that Sutter had tried some kind of funny business in the kitchen, or up in the maid quarters, or down in the laundry room, maybe shoving her back onto a pile of dirty sheets and fondling her, reaching up and under her skirt while she tried to fight back, feeling the shame and fear that came when a boy tried something with a girl, knowing that if she said anything her mother would lose her job. In later years he'd slip that into the story when they talked it over. As he aged, it seemed too much that he had beaten Sutter before he had learned the story. He had gone at Sutter not out of a sense of dignity or honor, or even because of the slight about being an Okie, and only after the fight—when the parking lot cleared and somehow he got close enough, caught up with her, tapped her shoulder, his face still bloody, his eyes bruised, and said hello, leaning forward, trying to wink but instead wincing, slightly confused somehow because she had the high, clean forehead and hairdo of a rich girl even though she wasn't—maybe he knew that much, understood that she was the daughter of the kind of woman who would do the Sutters' laundry. Who else but someone like her would appear at the end of a fight, in the lonely parking lot, and lend a hand, touching his cut and saying it needed to be stitched, simply standing there without fear at the sight of his battered face?

THE CHAIR

Day after day I went through the paternal motions, testing my son while he tested me, trying to teach him not only to do what I said, which seems like a given, but also to see and taste the world in certain ways, with an ideal in mind, a purified vision of the best way to live reduced to a rudimentary, five-year-old version: good eye contact with others, a sustained gaze, not just looking, but giving an indication of having seen—a head nod—and maintained long enough to show respect and not too much fear. I wanted to be assured that he wouldn't end up painfully shy. (He didn't.) I feared he'd grow into one of those in-the-corner wallflower types, dainty and delicate, brooding, ponderous, sad as a young kid and then sullen when he hit the teenage years and then, as an adult, deeply depressed. (He didn't.) I wanted him to open up to what was before him. So, I suppose, part of me—in the yard that afternoon, as I followed him up the hill—was happy that he was resisting my commands and remained slightly beyond reach. While, of course, another part of me was ready to pounce on him as soon as he turned at the top and headed down to the retaining wall again.

You're in the chair, little man, right now, get inside quick, the chair is waiting!

I prefer a gentle pushing against my will—I was thinking in the yard that afternoon, as I got near the top of the hill. By the time I got to the top, he had turned and was jogging slowly north toward the Thompsons' Scotch pines—the hiss, the high-up touch of wind in the crowns. Then he made a tight loop, wobbly with his legs in his jeans, with the cuffs rolled up, and his coat flapping (he refused to zip up, but I let that go), and, after glancing back at me, he pumped his arms up and down and screeched. To my right, the river beyond the wall stretched at least three miles across, with the ebb tide and the flood tide meeting in the center to form a sheen of calm. The autumnal brown and gold leaves on the Westchester side threw long reflections that blended with the sky. Ah, glorious, I thought. Ah, a lovely and perfect fall afternoon. The sublime nature of taking care of my boy on one more bygone day. There was a deep, submerged loneliness in my chest as I stood feeling the wind, which was lifting, growing firmer and stronger from the north, bringing with it the first hints of winter—along with the sound of the birds, who had flown deeper into the Thompsons' trees. Oh, the beauty of knowing that on that day I'd instruct the boy on how to listen carefully and establish proper eye contact, and on holding his little wee-wee straight when he peed into the bowl, and how to hold his fork and to take care with his chewing. Part of the glory of the moment, I think I thought, was in the pristine clarity of the innumerable potential teaching moments— Christ, I still despise that phrase!—that would bloom in the next few hours, as the light waned and the wind continued to lift and the remaining leaves twisted loose from their stems and were brushed away, skittering across the lawn, lying there, waiting to be blown away by the crew who would arrive midmorning on Saturday, four or five men, and lean down into the roar as their earmuffs snuffed them into a different kind of solitude. Evening would fall, and the lights on the bridge and across the river would throw themselves onto the surface of the water, appearing one by one as the sky faded, and then, safely inside the house, I'd look out the window and feel the fantastic unleashing of the pure, frank wistfulness that used to come to me at that time of day, and I'd feel, ahead, the future in one form or another, without which I could not endure the task. At some point in the future we'd be alone in the house and Gunner would be off at college, or married, and days like that would be sucked into a vortex— what other way to think of it?—of retrospect, with just a few memories of day-to-day tending: car-seat buckling, food feeding, punctuated by more pointed memories of trauma: stitches in his brow (lacrosse), asthma attack (holding him through the night, his tiny chest heaving against my palm), his separation problems at the preschool (me in the window watching him clutch hold of the old, scratched-up piano bench, his mouth wide open in a scream, his face bright red and shiny). It was only with that sense that I could survive those moments, I think I thought.

Reaching the top of the yard, I became aware—in a kind of intuitive parenthood tracking mode—that I'd already given him one warning and release and another solid warning. It's possible, I think I thought, that in the pleasure of running downhill, he had forgotten my first warning, which he never really let sink in, distracted by the sound of the birds in the trees (because he had turned to look at them), so that the second warning came to him as a first warning of sorts. I jogged behind him and kept the shadow/father distance and gave him space to decide what to do, wondering again if he'd just weave partway down, having absorbed my warning and then my second warning, which in theory nullified the first warning and showed my hypocrisy at not simply drawing the line and taking him inside, but figuring that another chance was warranted because it was possible that in his delight he simply forgot that first warning, but, on the other hand, I think I thought, this time he has at least two warnings echoing in his head, and so I held back on shouting to him again: If you run too close to the wall, it's the chair. Instead, I stayed quiet and thought about how just that morning I had gone down and looked out the window at the river and thought it was strange that in the last two weeks Sharon had come home late each night, arriving after dinner, appearing in the driveway with perfectly fine excuses, saying the train was late, or there was traffic on the bridge. (Did she not know that I could see the bridge and the traffic, and looked at it in a habitual manner most days, glancing over there when I went down to the shore to examine the wall, worrying over the fact that it was crumbling, wondering how much weight the grass and sod and soil made pushing against the structure while, at the same time, worrying over the potential cost of repair, imagining the mason digging it all out, building some kind of temporary support wall, laying new rebar, framing it up, and then somehow getting a cement truck—Concrete, Sharon corrected me when I verbalized my worry one night: not cement, it's concrete— down into the yard?) Other excuses she gave included irate clients, or long-winded partner conferences she had to attend because she was hell-bent on making partner as soon as possible. I'm hugely aware, I said, of the weird feeling I have about you and your work in relation to me and my position here as at-home caregiver, and sometimes I have to admit, I sit at the window and follow you to work in my imagination. Now, don't get me wrong, I cherish this time with Gunner and I'm happy to be doing this, but, still, I feel strange about it at times, I said, while she pursed her lips and fixed me with her gaze, which included really fine, deep, dark, big eyes in a face that was smooth with lean cheekbones and a fine, fine nose. A fucking Helen of Troy face, I used to think. The kind of face that would start a war if you let it. And it did, eventually. I'd like to start a war, I used to think, seeing her face. I want to start something big and historic in her name. I want a monument to be built in honor of the torment her face creates in my fellow men. (I think I sensed—those mornings of window gazing—that she was being sucked into Manhattan. The pull of it was apparent to me in the jaunt, the sway of her hips as she skipped out to the car each morning. It appeared in the way she held her chin softly in her fingers, splaying them out in a thoughtful manner as she listened to me describe my day while a slight—albeit graceful—incomprehension filled her eyes. All that beauty gave her a density that was prone to the pull of the city, I thought, I think.) Those mornings, with Gunner upstairs asleep—the soft sea-hiss snooze of his breath coming through the baby monitor—I sometimes had that deep, sensual foreboding that came when I thought too much about the short term and the way Gunner's days, still fresh and new, his life just starting, stood logarithmically in relation to my own thirty years. A day was one small fragment of my life, and a day for him was a much larger piece of the pie. One day now is a big hunk of his five years on earth, I used to think, I think.

On those mornings, with my cheek against the glass, I

imagined the soft rub of her attaché against her leg as she
waited on the station platform, filled with a communal sensation of being in on a secret—a united sense of waiting to head to
a common destination, and then on the train, with the attaché at her feet, the prim way she'd hold the paper, while over
her shoulder old boatyards—bright blue tarps—and track detritus roared past and the river itself stayed calm and passive,
blue on one day, gray on another. At the window, I anticipated
the solitude of the upcoming day with Gunner for company,
maybe some playtime with another kid and his mother, who
would stand awkwardly as the erotic charge failed to form between us, and because of that fact we'd feel even more awkward, aware that it should form, if not a spark then at least a
slight vibration of some sort as we watched and, on occasion,
shouted instructive bits of information: Be careful now, not so
hard, be nice, share, be good, Gunner, let her play with that.
Annie, come over here and let me tie your shoe, not so hard.
Or larger, more philosophical comments that covered the
gamut from sharing to being kind to each other to the way the
trees look against the sky, always pointing things out as a way
to teach looking, to make sure they were seeing, and then,
other times, encouraging them to find deeply imaginative
modes—this happened mostly with a mother named Grace,
who would instruct the kids to imagine elaborate pizza parlors, saying, Why don't you cook some pizzas for me and
Mr. Allison (Call me Bob, I'd say, please call me Bob) . . .

     . . . again, at the window those mornings I felt the
power of the city—all that culture and commerce compacted,
hemmed in on all sides by water, held in to create a force powerful enough to radiate all the way to our house, to the plot of
land and the town itself, which, I imagined, was just at the

edge of the force field, catching the last bits of energy before it was absorbed by the parkland to the north, the heavy stone palisades and trees on my side of the river, and, on the other side, the wide-open land and dirt roads and split-rail fences and horse stables and large estates in northern Westchester. (The field slides farther up on that side of the river, I thought at the window. There are fewer obstructions to dull its power over on that side.) At the window, I imagined Sharon entering her firm's building near Forty-Second Street, the glossy lobby with the security man up front watching as she swiped her card and the glass partition zipped neatly open and she felt a grandness that came from her ability to pass through, while behind her messengers and visitors waited to sign in at the desk, looking somewhat distracted, holding on their faces the placid perplexity of the scrutinized, some part of them worrying the idea that a day might come when suddenly, on a big delivery or an important appointment, they'd be denied entry.

During those morning window sessions, I imagined Sharon as she entered a loaded elevator with her colleagues and felt that New York elevator pride that comes with squeezing close without annoyance, moving up into a money-making venture of some sort, lifted into the coffee smell of the office space, the brief hello at the reception desk . . . I imagined . . . the lovely entanglement in a web of selfsame need, risk, and obligation. Behind me in the kitchen the coffee maker burbled and coughed.

We're riding on an apex, I thought standing in the yard that day, I think. We're on a pivot. On one side is her career and her lively step out the door, while on the other is this deep solitude, with the birds still chirping madly, startling each other into a frenzy of noise, each one simply responding to the others and the others responding in kind. The afternoon light was starting to wane slightly over the water, catching riffles far out as the smooth, wide, glossy patch near the center began to swirl itself away and waves worked themselves in, lapping the retaining wall. Then the birds seized up for a second, turned themselves into a fury of flapping, papery in nature, like long skeins of tissue being shaken out. I noticed all that as I turned to look at Gunner again. It's not that I feel sorry for myself in any way, because I cherish these moments with my boy, delight in being with him. I relish the line I have to walk between being loving and soft and coddling one second and the next having to reestablish my command, or, better yet, my guidance—a towering figure in his little mind—over his development at that particular point in time, I was thinking, I think. Love isn't in the actual grab and heft of body when he comes out of school and runs into my arms, crying with glee. No. Love is the moment just as he comes out the school-house door, standing amid his friends, and searches for my eyes. Love is in the second he sees me, and I see him, dressed in one of his outrageous outfits, bright stunning coats, weird hats, drooping strange pants (because we took delight in taking advantage of the fact that at that stage he had no idea what he was wearing, no sense of having to fit in, and we could get him dolled up—Sharon's words—as cute as a button). That's what love is, I thought each time I went to the school to pick him up. Then, as I lifted him and felt his weight, the purity of the moment vanished and I would smell the stale, tart odor under his collar while he smelled, I suppose, the smoke and coffee on my breath and something else that later, at some point, perhaps even in memory, he would recognize as the first hints of decay.

The birds flew over the water and got about a quarter of the way across the river and then, suddenly, swooped in a wide arc back around toward the Thompsons' trees again, catching up with each other in a teardrop, diverting me from Gunner, who, when he caught my attention again, was striking straight for the wall and the water. His tiny, shrill cries mixed with the wind. In the compressed intensity of the moment, the birds were gone. The tide had shifted, heading down toward the city.

You're getting the chair, I said, stop. No more warnings, I yelled as I charged down the hill. He was way ahead of me, of course, and in a moment he'd be at the wall and starting— naturally—his tiptoe tightrope walk along the structure, testing his own sense of balance and fear as it relates to the drop and the water below. (In the summer I'd lower him down to the beach, feeling his shoulder and joints and tiny chest at the tip of my fingers. Then we'd sit on an old pickle bucket and fish.) In a moment he'd be looking back at me, I was thinking, the wind in my hair, feeling, as I moved, a good, manly sense of dominion over everything. This is mine, I was thinking, I think. This is my chance at glory of a sort, perhaps I was thinking. I don't remember. But he was at the wall, wobbling along, and then he tumbled backward, throwing his arms up in the air.

That's it, I said. That's it, Gunner. No more warnings. (Half thinking that perhaps this was actually my fourth warning, and that he'd long forgotten the first one, a few hours ago, before we went to preschool.) Across the river on the Westchester side, a train charged up the tracks like a sliver of glass, and when the wind died I heard not only Gunner's giggles, as he swayed, but also the deep rumble of the diesel express that would go past Ossining, past Croton, and all the way up to Poughkeepsie, and I felt, hearing it, a sorrow that came not only of my inability to get to him on time but also something much deeper—I'd later think—that had to do with the fact that as he fell over the wall, he fell back with his eyes wide, terrorized by the way his balance had defied him.

Then I got to the wall and looked down and saw that the tide was still coming in and he was lying on his side in a few inches of water, with a shawl of wet, black sand around his collar, and his socks muddy, and his eyes guilty but also comic, looking up at me, establishing a long, sustained moment of good eye contact. Keep looking, I thought. Don't ever stop. Continue to look at me like that for the rest of time, I think I thought. Then the fear that had begun to form when I was halfway down the yard caught up, pure, sharp, and eternal in form, and struck me under the rib bone. I was weeping softly as I lowered myself down to help him, lifting my palms and supporting his feet so he could clamber over the wall.

Then he stood atop it and looked down at me, his old man, as I wiped my eyes. He was looking down at a bright red face, bewhiskered and ruddy. A mouth moving on that face was saying, That's it. You're in the chair. It's the chair for you, little man. No snack. Just the chair. I mean it. I gave you three, at least, maybe four warnings, the mouth kept saying. You're damn lucky the tide wasn't all the way up. Meanwhile, the day had folded into itself and combined with the terror to become vivid and pristine and perfect. Across the river the train was gone.

Then, as the wind roared along the Palisades at Hook Mountain and took on a northerly bite, as night began to descend upon the water and the tidal flow established itself in a southerly direction, working firmly past the bridge pylons, churning up white Vs, my son leaned and offered his hands to help me over the wall, and the air between us, before we actually touched, filled with an astonishingly pure love. It was there for a few seconds, and then it vanished and I took him into the house to the chair, where I told him to sit until Sharon came home.

He resisted, squirming from the chair, but I insisted, saying, Sit there and wait until your mother gets home. Your time's not up. Your time's not even close to being up.

THE TERMINAL ARTIST

At the time, her death had seemed in the order of the way things sometimes go, when bad luck and the physiological nature of the trauma—in this case swelling of the brain after cancer surgery—combine to betray the curative efforts of the medical establishment. We mourned her death as a natural event. Right away (even the day we got the news) we felt her absence as a part of the wider—again natural—scheme of the world. She had simply gone the way other living things go, succumbing to the frailty of biological systems. The cancer had been excised in a clean and sharp procedure, but then another factor had come into play. This is not to say that the loss wasn't great, but in the end her death seemed part of yet another beautiful tragedy. What was hoped for and what happened were at odds. Her children—two young daughters—would never have a mother, and her wonderful voice—she sang in a gospel group—would never be heard again. For a few months our grief continued to sharpen and then, day by day, it tapered off until what we could remember about her—that lively, light laugh, her lovely eyes—began to erase the painful day of her burial. Six years later the Terminal Artist—as the media dubbed him—confessed to having killed patients in an upstate hospital. He had tweaked the medication on several post-op patients (always doing so in a professional manner: easing them over the line with clinical care, never just simply pulling a plug or drowning them in ridiculous amounts of morphine. He performed mercy killings that were meant, he claimed, to save—his words—a world of suffering). When he came to light, the hospitals and insurance companies were forced to review cases and slowly, over the course of several months, began to solve the mystery of several deaths that had been attributed to natural causes. Perfectly fine post-op cases, young men and women with strong physical constitutions and powerful wills, with the odds on their side, often came out of anesthesia, lived a few days, and then died quietly in the middle of the night, resisting heroic efforts before they fell into the void forever. While the so-called Terminal Artist was busy admitting that he had killed four or five patients in an upstate hospital, authorities went back and traced the history of his employment to ten institutions that had eagerly hired him over a fifteen-year period because not only was he a nurse, in high demand at the time, but a male nurse to boot. Not only a male nurse but a highly trained one, highly personable, with a clean-shaven, tidy disposition and a voice that was pleasant, calm, and bright. The kind of man you would want at your bedside, thoughtful and considerate while at the same time efficient and orderly. One of those careful chart checkers and hand washers. A man who probably lived a somewhat lonely, austere, bachelor life, working the long hours the job required out of a dedication to the profession. I'm a mercy provider, he explained in court a year later. I dole out mercy. I ease burdens. I vanquish pain. I help provide a smooth transition to the afterlife. I'm obligated to God. I do God's work. The Lord is in my heart. His will be done. I end lives to provide salvation. Only mercy, all the time. He went on like this until the judge put his hand up and ordered him to stop.

At the hospitals where he had worked, those cases that had been most certainly natural, a part of the order of the natural world, became automatically suspect. Whereas certain cases, at least the ones that he had admitted to outright, about ten, maybe fifteen, and a few others, were immediately reclassified as homicides. Each (confessed) death (suddenly) had an exact cause: a micromanaged drip of morphine, just enough to induce a heart failure that looked somewhat natural; an extra dose of digoxin that sent a patient—just out of open-heart surgery—tumbling over the life-death line in a way that looked to be a matter of simple physiology. With pride in his voice, he spoke of providing mercy with the application of what he called calibrated pushes, nudges that simply served to augment what otherwise were perfectly natural (his phrase) situations, so that, for example, the muscles of the heart, already tired and weak after being put into a holding action, released their energies and gave up in a way that was a relief to their fibers (he said); or in the case of a young child who was in an induced coma, simply allowing her to continue her journey to God instead of allowing her to rebound back into a life of earthly hell. All of this just to say that when my friend died, after brain surgery, in a small hospital in upstate New York, when Cherie died in the dead heart of a wintry night, alone, in a room in the intensive care ward; when her brain swelled in a postoperative condition and the unrelieved pressure somehow—this is pure speculation—caused her heart to fail later the next day, it was originally chalked up to an act of God, if you believed, or just one more natural failure of the body. One more tragic cancer death that left behind three children and a father and an empty silence beyond reckoning. It seemed to be the type of death that allowed only a certain vantage, because to get too close to it, to home into the loss, would be to touch a kind of madness and to admit that there was only raw chance and nothing else involved, and to fully admit to that would—at least for me—be to give in to the purest kind of terror. All I could do at that point was try to get as close as possible to the elemental loss: mourn her absence; remember her lean, lovely face and soft laugh; pray, or not pray, that her soul would live on in one form or another, if not up in some heavenly place then at least in those who held memories of her life here. But then, six years later, a story appeared in the media that the abovementioned Terminal Artist had been caught, or tracked down through careful scrutiny of two similar cases in the same upstate hospital. Many, hearing the word *upstate*, couldn't help visualizing a series of particular images: cracked roads swaying along the Hudson River, which is always hidden down behind an overgrown verge; wide fields of weeds and grass leading to the second-growth forest that has overtaken whatever agriculture once flourished up there, if it ever did; rusted factories leaching PCBs into the river. The upstate of the imagination begins just about where the salt front, the upmost reach of the flood tide coming up from New York Harbor, ends in Newburgh Bay. (My image of upstate has been shaped by the photographs of Richard Prince: abandoned clapboard houses, rust-smeared trailer homes, silent—also rusted—basketball hoops, roads with skid marks left by the obligatory rites of bored teenagers who find solace in jack-starting cars, fishtailing dramatic 360s. Muscle cars, power-ful beyond everyday need, shudder outrageously while the long, lean contours of their hoods—glossed to a high polish—stretch out to lick the bleak horizon.)

The Terminal Artist, never venturing south of Newburgh, worked the second-tier hospitals that formed a constella-tion of upstate New York medical care stretching all the way to Buffalo, which somehow escapes the upstate tag by being along the shore of Lake Ontario, which for its part touches the shore of Canada. All this just to say that the fact that he worked in upstate hospitals seems to resonate retroactively with the region itself and the fact that so many—not all, but many—of its population already suffered, and so had to suffer doubly from his actions. The assumption—in the media—was that his victims, by virtue of being cared for in hospitals upstate, actu-ally lived upstate. This wasn't the case. Cherie was living in a small Hudson River town about thirty miles upstream from Manhattan when she had a divine vision in which God told her—she explained this to her friends shortly before the operation—to seek out Dr. Drake, a stout neurosurgeon with a prim manner and a few brain operations under his belt.

In any case, outside the hospital on that cold winter night was a landscape somewhat dismal, lonely, silent, abject, and sad, struggling mightily to hold up against tough economic times, working hard to shrug off a stigma that came from being beyond the cultural gravity field of the great city downstream. (In all honesty, until I got word of the Terminal Artist, I held the entire region complicit in her death.) For a long time after I got the news about the Terminal Artist, I found it hard to believe that this dear friend of mine had succumbed to a complex array of chances, an infinite range of factors that had combined to put her in a particular bed, in a particular hospital, to have a particular form of surgery, to solve a particular medical problem, and in doing so met with a particular ward nurse, who happened to have been on duty that particular night, and who had a particular derangement, or sense of obligation to a particular concept of mercy, and administered a dose of some particular, albeit unknown, substance (the case is still open). Most found it nearly impossible to grasp the complex factors that had vectored together to put her life into the hands of a madman. When news of the Terminal Artist broke, her death was six years in the past, not much more than a blip of pain, an old memory that included the day I got word of her death, one dreary afternoon at the cabin upstate (not really upstate, at least theoretically: a small cabin near Goshen, not far from the Wallkill River, a place to hang my hat when I'm out in my waders—and somehow that stretch of river, drawing a wide array of rather rich folks from the city and suburbs, seems protected from the various associations one has with the term *upstate*); just sitting reading Isaac Babel while the baby dozed and Irene took a catnap; nothing but a kind of deep silence—not even the murmur of the fridge, maybe the wind sweeping through the strand of pines at the end of the property. Then my phone rang and my father-in-law, a doctor himself, went into it carefully, speaking in his precise medical voice, sticking with the facts: She had died overnight, deep in the night, the time not exactly known, had succumbed to heart failure after swelling of the brain and so on and so forth. That memory—the deep white hiss, maybe, of wind through the trees and the baby's soft snoring, not so soft actually, really a rather loud sound to be coming from a six-month-old girl. That memory merged with memories of the funeral, a vast affair in a big domed church that had once been a music hall: everyone in white, except for those of us who had come up from the city, and the women wearing pants (those who weren't were provided with wide linen napkins to cover their knees for the sake of modesty, I suppose). The entire service had a tone of jubilation, of joy and replenishment based on the idea, maybe the concept—no, much deeper, the knowledge—that she had passed forth into some much better realm; that she had been provided with a direct trip into heaven, so to speak. The tone was assured, brilliantly bright— with her own gospel group singing rapturously while we confused city folks tried to ride with it in an agreeable manner, holding our own as much as possible, trying not to draw judgments because her African American culture rubbed up against our whiteness and we, as whites, assumed the privilege of assuming we had no real ethnicity, just a void that was— I'm guessing here—the norm—tried hard to imagine our way into their attitudinal stance: painful joy over the foreordained status of being offered up into some holy receivership that was visualized as pearly gates, perhaps, wide-open arms, holy, draped in white. All this—in memory—was six years in the past when the news broke of the Terminal Artist's confession (case still open) and sparked a turning back to old memories that had been blurred and tarnished by time—and perhaps amplified: the smell of the lavender perfume of the woman who escorted us to our seats. Her father's large morose face— beading with sweat as he sang. The delusional notions of the Terminal Artist, who claimed he'd been helping his patients along the path to heaven, blended with the jubilation at the funeral over the fact that she had made the trip to heaven and was at the feet of her holy maker, or through the pearly gates, or already up there in some cloudy realm, cottony and light.

There was that long period of time when we had no knowledge of the Terminal Artist, those beautiful days when we carried a sorrow born—we thought—out of somewhat natural processes. Not man-made sorrow. (Going down to the river I was still thinking. *Man-made?* That phrase is all I hold to because the rest of it—the interminable series of chances, the long retrospective chain of incidents, from the fact that she got cancer at that particular time, or at least spotted it, to her deciding upon that particular hospital, out of some deep religious idea, maybe [too many factors to name, I thought, heading down to the river, wading through the brush, the overgrowth of wild bamboo and thicker brambles to the stream edge], while, at the same time, the so-called Terminal Artist had moved from one hospital to the next, taking advantage of the high demand for nurses, moving from one upstate hospital to another, and then to a hospital in Lancaster for a few months before heading back upstate, leaving a trail of dead behind—seemed too much to ponder.)

·

In my work, I've described the way it feels to step into the icy water with waders on while the rubber compresses your legs. The odd sensation of stepping with felt bottoms onto the slick stones and toeing along, always somewhat fearful of the plunge into the unknown but secure somehow after years of doing it, able to sense the dangers. I've used fishing as metaphor, but never shamefully. I've used the swayback motion of the cast, the old-fashioned basics of tying the fly to the line. Once again I've turned to it because in the strange solitude at the center of the river, with the water flowing on both sides, I feel grateful that at least for six years we were able to think of her death as natural. I'd never be able to use her death in a story. I'd have to find some other way, I thought, and then once again I unleashed a cast and once again watched the line spread itself neatly across the surface so that the fly, at the end of the tapered leader, was invisible, sunk in the glimmer of light, floating ahead—one more image making me alive to that particular moment, with the hard, cold surge of flow all around me, floating beautifully along on an infinite number of chance vortices. But of course that day on the stream is six years old, and the funeral itself is six years behind that, so that twelve years have passed since our friend died and six since we got the news about the Terminal Artist. Six years have passed, and the story of the Terminal Artist has faded from public memory and been replaced by other, more current and therefore seemingly more urgent narratives, so that all we can do, each day, is hold on to the hope of finding an attendant structure that might begin somehow, on a cold fall afternoon, in a hospital room, perhaps, or maybe out in the parking lot during a smoking break, when the killer nurse (dubbed the Terminal Artist) takes in the air and relishes the beauty of the afternoon breeze, bringing with it a briny sea smell of the river's ebb tide. There is a pristine blue sky overhead, and across the street the leaves have changed on the trees, spilling brilliant colors into the air. Everything is hard and bright. He is thinking carefully about his next move, deliberate and thoughtful. There is the glory of God in the air, he thinks. He shuffles his feet a little bit and flicks his cigarette into the curb. He is eager to get in and get started. He has work to do. Good, hard work. Then he bows his head and says a little prayer, offering his services directly to the Lord, just like Abraham did up on the mountaintop, clearheaded and unconfused, with his son in his arms awaiting the knife, offering up his soft, smooth neck for the moment at hand.

FATHERHOOD: THREE

THE PROBLEMATIC FATHER

The problem is, my son sees the man I am now and not the men I was before I became the man I am now. The man I am now is a result of *his* presence in my life and therefore I'm not even close to being the man I was before he existed, and *that* man, it seems, had a pure vitality that was taken away by the responsibilities that arrived with his son's birth. On the other hand, the father I knew was the father who was there when I was there, and so the fact that my father was highly problematic at times came in part from the fact that he was dealing with me. But then the fact that being a father means having a son, or a daughter, must also mean that without a son or daughter one cannot be a father, and so, of course, the vital man who existed without the son or daughter wasn't a father. Therefore, whatever he was before the son or daughter existed doesn't count and can't be compared with the man he became once he was a father. The father I know is the man who had to deal with a mentally ill daughter. During those first several years he didn't know she was mentally ill and was, at that time, simply a man who had a daughter who was in trouble all the time. Then, later, he became the father of a mentally ill daughter, which changed the way he looked at things but not her troubles—she was still arrested, disappeared for months at a time, had to be rescued from one scenario to the next, including a court case that lasted six weeks when she was sixteen; then jail time, and later, the stolen checks she cashed, more jail time, and mental hospitals, and so on and so forth. The father I remember is most often the later, older father who had to figure out ways to deal with an older mentally ill daughter. He was a problematic man, but heroic in his own way. Now here I am, a father with a son and daughter who can only see me the way I am now, I thought. I thought: There is nothing I can do but present myself as best I can to my son and daughter as a man who is aware that he is not as vital—or alive—as he was before he had a son or daughter, or perhaps alive in a different way, as a father, and in doing so give them something that other men, who don't even think about these things, might be missing. In that manner, I might avoid being a problematic father. Although just by thinking about it so much—not only my own relationship with my son and daughter but also how I saw my father as a man who was dealing with a troubled daughter, and later a mentally ill daughter—I'm exposing myself as a problematic father.

THE SAD SACK

On the train in the dead of winter, I looked out at the water and saw a man in a kayak, his paddle flashing in the morning sun as he worked hard, looking forlorn and silent, trying to dig against the tide. He was a doomed man, I thought. One way

or another, no matter what kind of shape he was in, even if
he got to shore and hauled his boat up, scraping the ice off
the sides, lovingly rubbing her hull with a cloth before going
inside to heat his hands alongside a stove, the fire simmering
and comforting, sipping coffee while he looked out triumphantly
at the river, he would be unable to detect in his groin the upcoming events that would, some other day, in similar conditions, when he was just as strong and sure of himself, take
him to task with a rogue barge wake, striking his kayak from
the side, startling him forever out of his mute complacency
until he was nothing more or less than a man clinging to a hull.
Call me deranged or a sad sack, but that's what I imagined
when I caught sight of him before the train entered the tunnel
and a surge of ear-popping darkness threw his image against
the soft agony of my own life. That's the way I thought back
then. Even a beautiful sight—a man alone on the river bearing up against the elements, daring nature—delivered to me a
sense of doom.

(ANOTHER) STORY I'D LIKE TO WRITE

A man who has been married twenty-five years remembers the
time his son broke his femur in the backyard—twilight drifting in the trees—by catching his heel in a hole in the grass,
falling at an odd angle, spiraling the bone. I'd like to write
about cradling my crying son, his shoulders quivering as we
drove him to the hospital. Not in order to show how pain and
love combine in a particularly vivid fashion—no, not that!—
but rather in order to explore the way heart and touch unite
under duress. I'd recall the hefty, stiff weight of his body as I
carried him out of the hospital to the car. In his cast—on both

legs—he felt like a gift, a Yule log, and my wife and I knew, weary and exhausted after the ordeal, the shock of seeing the femur split down the middle on the X-ray, that we'd be in for a long, hot summer. I'd like to get in the story how it felt to be a man who could bear up under certain responsibilities. I'd like to capture that particular afternoon, when my son found a way to translate his inability to an ability, not even understanding that he was limited, because for all he knew, it seemed, his state at that point in time was simply one more stage he had to go through, like a pupa in a cocoon, as he threw his arms wide and made a swimming motion, pushing himself across the sunlit floor through the motes of dust and the quiver of leaf shade as he made a light, half-laughing hoot sound to accompany each stroke while we held hands and looked down and watched and felt at that particular moment that we had everything under control and were operating under the auspices of a deep wisdom that seemed to arrive just often enough to allow us to negotiate each day, one at a time, as a visionary end goal: a full-grown man who would function on his own in the world, using what he had garnered from us to confront whatever the future threw his way. If I could get even a fraction of this down in some kind of pure form, I would be able to lean back, rest, and simply live in the world.

FAREWELL, MY BROTHER

On the edge of the parking lot, the man named Frankie was with them, just hanging out, scuffing the ground, grunting, laughing, putting the halfway house behind them for a moment and looking out through the trees at the river, dark with flecks of light. Frankie's a sea-dog type, all hunch and roll of shoulders. He tapped his watch cap with his index finger, making his habitual salute gesture. He's one of those who came lumbering out of the vapor, his sway and his sea-dog talk marking him as an anomaly. He claimed to have been unreadable to the punks up in Newburgh, saying: I bought and sold quick at a profit. Gangs all around me, I mean violence day to day with guys killing each other over corner turf, until I stepped into the void opened by the dead, found my business footing, and ran an operation until, a year later, they stopped killing each other, combined forces, and called my name in to the DEA tip line. That was all it took. Judge offered me a plea, so long as I fingered a few. I complied and he put me in the clink for a few months. As a matter of fact I was in Sing Sing, right across the river. I was lucky because that judge had a sense of my future potential. He read it in my eyes. I presented myself as sober and clean, and that's what he saw when he looked. Newburgh's one of those towns—the rest of the country don't give a shit so long as it stays out of sight, you see. He touched his watch cap whenever he paused. After I came east from Duluth, before I ended up in Newburgh, I worked a stint on a harbor tug, meeting big ships coming in. There's nothing like the tedium of waiting for the meet-and-greet to bring some tanker, loaded to the hilt, into the bosom of the harbor, he said. Those big container ships couldn't make a move into New York Harbor without our guidance, and that's what gave us so much power, you see, because until they unloaded their goods they were simply hauling potential profit, which is depressing as all hell and makes the heart sink. So we'd hang back and hide in the fog while they signaled like mad . . . He rambled on, while the others looked through the trees at the dark glint of water and maintained the studied, blasé posturing of men who'd been detoxed in local hospital wards, sent to the Blaisdell unit of Rockland Psychiatric or down to Bellevue and then out again, and were now sneaking smokes—against Open Embrace regulations—four days before Christmas. They listened with respect to Frankie, in part because his stories sounded reasonably truthful. Straight-up, truthful stories—they all knew and agreed silently—were a rare find. As Frankie said: You get intense heat at the bottom of a very large pile of bullshit, you see, and in the smithy of that heat a few of the words congeal and solidify and become diamonds of truth, bright enough to send shafts of light through the cracks.

On this night the Hudson was frozen along the shore, and the soft *shish* of ice sliding over itself as the tide swept up-

stream, or down, became audible when the traffic noise on
the road behind them subsided. The men had been talking
for half an hour. The one nicknamed Esquire had grown
quiet. He'd made the mistake of trying to play the pity card,
explaining that he'd lost his law practice, his wife, his little girl
Abigail, and so on, while the men, absorbing the frankness
in his voice, emitted a brutal vibe that said, We're not going
into that bullshit compare-and-contrast mode. We're done
with that for now. We're out here simply to break a minor rule, so
that if we're caught, by Ron or whoever's on shift tonight,
we're caught together. Who's on shift? someone mumbled.
Christ, I don't know or give a damn, the man named Bernard
said. He was gaunt and stiff-jointed and extremely thin, even
for a rehabbed junkie pushing into his late sixties.

All five men—I imagined—were keenly sensing that this
moment, as much as any other, might prove to be the one that
sparked their demise, just like the last time they'd touched a
bottle to their lips, or shot the needle in, or snorted a line from a
tabletop. What held them together, as they shared cigs from
Frankie's pack, was the fact that long ago, years back, the rules
of the world had shifted and they'd learned that even clean and
sober they'd get cheated out of something. The only one in
the group who didn't feel this way was Alex, one of Frankie's
roommates, who was a first-timer, fresh out of his initial
rehab stint at Good Samaritan and still feeling a newborn
cleanliness that, the men understood, was as dangerous as
anything. (It's like a clean chalkboard, man, Frankie had said.
Remember that. Like when you'd get to class before the teacher
and see that chalk, and that clean board, and you'd write some
nasty words on it before she came in. You see, Alex, that's what
you are. Your brain is pretty much a clean board, and the chalk

is whatever drug's going to come along next. You're going to want to write on that board, and you're probably going to do it because you're still just a kid. And if you don't do it, some lug like me will come along and do it for you. And who are you? Alex had said. I'm a boatswain, Frankie said. I'm a gob full of the wisdom that comes from being trapped on a Great Lakes freighter for months at a time. Every ship I served on back in the day had someone the likes of you, a newbie with meat on his bones staggering around with a bunch of cold carcasses, sun- and wind-bleached and washed up on the shore of duty—bolting hatches, scouring the taconite dust out of the hold. You'll find someone like me in every one of these half-way joints, he said. Believe me, you don't know it now but you'll go out to sea in one form or another and come back here just like me: a man who did deckhand duty on a Great Lakes freighter—after 'Nam, I should add—and got his sea legs and then went ashore and spent years wobbling around Duluth, sleeping nights at the Hope Mission, taking shore work when I could find it, but never forgetting my time on the ships, always able to recall the details, as you'll hear, my friend, because I tend to tell stories, not for the sake of elucidation, but because they're ingratiating, at least I think they are, when told properly. He'd gone on talking in the dark room, doing his best to cut through the new-roommate tension, while Alex stared at the ceiling and repressed a desire to push the window up and sneak off. [He'd do just that a few days later.] On that first night, as he lay back in his bed and listened to the old man talk, he was just starting to become aware of the big circle that arched over all these men. [You got to step out of the circle, Anne liked to say. She was rough in speech and large in girth and gave the same pre-session talks each time, leaning into the words with her husky voice, swaying slightly side to side, lifting her arms up, saying: You got to locate the circle, you sees, you got to locate it in the mind's eye and then step out of it in the mind's eye before it sweeps you around again. But sweet Jesus, you got to keep it in the mind's eye, she'd always add. You get it out of the mind's eye means you dead. All I'm sayin' is don't disregard the mind's eye. Keep the circle in it but stay off the circle. You heard me say all this before and you're gonna hear me say it again and again because it's so true it has to be said, and if I don't say it, it'll still be the truth, but it'll be the truth that hasn't been spoke, and that's a dangerous kind of truth, if you know what I'm sayin'. Then she'd go on to tell the story of her car breaking down on the Cross Bronx, with a dead engine and the wild traffic roaring past. A big black woman taking her skirt off to signal motorists for help, waving it above her head in a frantic way because her cell phone was dead and it was all she could think to do. You all don't have a good battery in the phone, no matter how fine the damn thing might be, no matter what quality, it don't work. In case you boys don't get the gist of what I'm sayin', your brain is the battery, your body is the phone, she'd say.])

Four months had passed since Alex's first night. All five men on the edge of the parking lot behind Open Embrace had arrived at a symbiotic balance, each one knowing the others as well as possible, at least as templates, as basic entities that were highly predictable and static in most ways. At least it felt that way. A keen sense of destiny lay between them and they knew that upon his release Frankie would head upstate again to score, slipping back into the Newburgh gang scene. Alex would sneak out the window a few times over the course of the months, risking ejection to see a girl, meeting her up at the tracks, hiking along to find a secluded spot. He'd fall into a routine, lifting the window gently, legging himself out onto the front porch, sneaking off, and then he'd get betrayed by the ease of it. He'd trust his luck until it came around to kick him in the ass.

Otherwise, on this night, not long before Christmas, the men settled into a stately quietude as they smoked and looked out at the water and heard the ice hiss. It was a pure silence—with the house behind them—in which they kept still, unwilling to scuff the pavement, or to kick the curb, and it would last about a minute. Then they'd shuffle and grunt and clear throats and spit and relight cigarettes and begin mumbling about Ron, who was inside decorating the joint, hanging lights in the meeting room.

As soon as the moment of quietude was over—the moment itself seemed to say to me—tensions would reform. Nothing could hold them in this state, and as they stood and breathed and puffed into the bitter air, another train, an express, warned the Ossining station with a long moan that came across the water and tried hard, but failed, to fill each one of them with a forlornness. Day and night these train horns passed through the fabric of life at Open Embrace mostly unnoticed, but on occasion one would enter a consciousness—usually an express, which was louder and more sustained but at the same time distant enough to have that mournful lost quality when heard in bed, or during a sudden cessation of confession in a group meeting, with a taint of abject potential, reminding the men of their own lack of industry. (Only Alex, who'd hopped a few trains, could hear that horn late at night and feel the inherent freedom in the sound.) In front of the house and up the little hillside, on the tracks along the western shore, only freights rumbled through, long rattling lines of cars, the couplings riding up against each other and then stretching out, headed up to Bear Mountain and then on to Albany. (You could easily load some bombs on that and take out West Point, Frankie liked to say. You just do a police flag of the engine, point a gun, hop aboard, and ride that baby straight into the heart of future army command. What I wouldn't pay to see some of those cadets wasted. It was one of them guys, fresh out of the Point, man, who got my best friend killed in Hue. But I'll spare you that fucking story for now. I'll save that one for later. I'll find a better time to lay that all on the line. I'll hold it until the moral of the story will sit in your heads for the rest of your fucking lives.) So the train horn tried as hard as it could to destabilize this moment of pure quietude. It tried to spark Frankie, who would sometimes think about the ore trains at Taconite Harbor, and the huge industrial contraption that allowed for entire cars to spill their loads into the holds, one after another. But on this night, with Christmas right over the horizon, he let the sound slip around the edges of his awareness. (I'm a shipman, he'd say. Never bought into that romantic nonsense about railroading. If I'm gonna drift I'm gonna really drift, if you know what I mean. If I'm inclined to floating atop something I'd rather it be on water than spiked to the earth.)

Did they feel the compression of the moment as they regarded the view? It wasn't simply that they shared a flash of cosmic isolation, a fleeting pause in the chaotic grumble of their existence. It wasn't simply that they seized intuitively upon that moment, knowing that when it ended they would turn and trudge back up to the house, unwilling to push their

luck with another cigarette because Ron had a pattern to the
way he worked. He'd come out and look off the back porch in
a few minutes. He'd take a break from putting up the mistletoe, which would cause problems later that night when Alex
would unknowingly stand beneath it and end up saying:
Fuck off, man, gross, while the other men said: You gotta pay
the price if you stand under the mistletoe, man.

   (They might say: He's the type who makes much of the
way things are and yet doesn't see the way they are because
he's so busy trying to see that he misses. They might say: He's
trying to purge the pain he feels about his beloved brother,
who, you know, went over the edge and began serious opiates
after smoking pot daily for years, just slipping off in middle
age until he lost his wife, his kids, his house along the Hudson,
not too far from Open Embrace, and his dog. He hauled his
brother around the town of Haverstraw, collecting his
worldly belongings in big contractor bags, putting them into
the shed behind the halfway house, and then, months later,
in the spring, took them out again when his brother was ejected
the first time for testing a big positive, because he'd gone down
to the river with a friend from Open Embrace and, seeing the
water and walking where he used to walk with his little boy,
the urge came, along with the opportunity, and he fell off the
wagon. [Man, his brother liked to say. That's still the best
fucking metaphor. That's it, man. We don't use wagons anymore. We don't even know what they are. But falling off them
is what we do best.])

•

(They might say: He's drawing inspiration from his brother,
who's now in Brooklyn, alone, solitary, out of phone contact,

perhaps alive, perhaps not—and in doing so shifting the onus of real life onto the lives of men he hardly knows, and in doing so projecting a hopeful moment of grace [if that's what it was] or agape [as Bernard would have it] onto a pause in the murmur of their talk, as witnessed one night just before Christmas. They might say: Who is he to draw so much from a single moment while the rest of the world roils and rolls forward; while the trains dig up and down the shoreline, like needles, carrying working men and women in and out of Manhattan; while the great, seething metropolis twenty-five miles downstream chugs on unknowingly, carelessly, with a blatant glory? Who is he to take a moment between a few fuckup men on the edge of a parking lot and pin it to the great spin of the cosmos, to the circular nature of addictive conditions that, at that particular moment, seemed to stop completely?

And I might say: Who are you to deny these men their moment of pure quietude? Who are you to withhold from them this one moment of pure collegial grace, just because you've never paused to listen raptly to the sound of ice—those long sheets creeping over one another as the tide ebbs, or floods, and the salty line shifts up the estuary from the abyssal plain at the far end of the Hudson Canyon? Or even imagined ice glistening like mica as it encroaches upon the shore, while up the river—past the silent, looming Bear Mountain Bridge, or farther up, past the Point, all the way into the depreciated reaches of Newburgh itself—the water, under a clear winter night, flash-freezes into a thick mass, packed into the bed like cotton against an abscessed tooth, and the men on the Coast Guard icebreaker, still up near Hyde Park, huddle on deck, sipping coffee, looking out, while the prow cuts a path? Just because you've never stopped to look up at the milky marl of sky as it purges the stars over Broadway, or down at the chewing gum nubs on the subway platform amid the smell of the third-rail ozone, doesn't mean that these men, a few days before the holiday, should be refused a single moment of grace, imaginary or real, as they waited for Ron, who, when he came to the door holding a string of Christmas bulbs, told me my brother was out back.)

•

Once they snapped out of the moment, they'd perceive the soft, residual sense of having been, briefly, united by some spirit that went beyond them, and they'd resent it and feel tense about it and even guilty because of the way it had been diminished. Frankie would repress the urge to begin talking of his deckhand days, holding the story he so badly wanted to tell for later, after the mistletoe fight, when there would be a sit-down meeting at which Ron would lecture them to no end about what it meant to fight over such silly things, and how they had to learn—if they were going to step out into the larger world—to negotiate situations. (He'd press hard on that word; he was a big one for situations. This situation or that. You'll find yourself in this situation and it'll be a situation that regards itself as something else—I mean a setup, or a fix—but look, men, you've got to see that anything you might step into, I mean outside, when you're clean, without the crutch of your substance of choice to lean on, will look like one more fuckup waiting to happen, but what you have to do, my friends, is to step back, gain a vantage, and look down from afar. I mean you'll have to go out-of-body, and then float over and scrutinize it carefully—and when you do that, I mean if you do it, men, you'll see a situation that can be controlled, like a signal-

man in a switch tower guiding rolling stock. [Ron claimed
to have worked as a signalman for the Burlington Northern,
throwing switches by simply pushing a button. Not a lever, he
said, but just this little fucking button that lit a light on an array and told you what was going on a few thousand miles away
in the real yard, which in this case was actually in Omaha, but
you still—and we were trained to do this—had to imagine
yourself on location in the yard with hundreds of boxcars sitting with their couplings spread. You still had to see the whole
setup, all the tracks, and know the manifests and so on and
so forth . . . He'd trail off as his faltering mind tried to locate
the rudiments of the job and avoid the truth that he'd been the
main key figure in a big pileup that had destroyed a million
dollars of fuel oil, lit up the sky for a hundred miles, and earned
a thirty-second spot on CNN. The fact that the explosion had
killed two men came from a Google search Alex made later.
Ron went pale when he heard the news and said: If it happened that way, the way you said, then I'm sorry for it. But
only the old Ron is sorry. The new, sober Ron feels just a hint
of the remorse he'd feel if he heard about anyone who happened to die in a stupid mishap.]) Frankie even had a sense of
the kind of fight that would break out. It would transpire
around the mistletoe—he speculated—and it would start with
a lighthearted jocularity, as a joke, and then quickly escalate,
after the kiss—because there was always a kiss involved—into
a tense standoff. The kissed man would wipe his mouth dra-
matically, using his sleeve, and then his hand. The kissed man
would spit on the ground and say: What the hell. You got no
right to do that to me, and the kisser would point up and say:
What the fuck do you think that is, parsley? And the kissee
would say: I don't care if that's fresh dope, man, you've got

no right to come into physical contact with me. (The kissee would, naturally, as a result of the kiss, find a flustered formality in his diction. He'd attempt to gain a foothold in pride, thinking of all the times he really had kissed a girl, gently touching his lips to those of another with an intent and hope that it would open up to more touching and then even love in some carnal manifestation, if he were lucky. All the men had been kissed weirdly, in bars, huddled down in some drainage ditch, side by side for warmth, sleeping soundly and awakening to a dreamy sensation—some kisser using sleep as an excuse, saying he didn't know what he was doing. Most of the men, and even the kid, Alex, had fought close to death with some other fuckhead, getting into a clench, only to find the man near at hand, just inches away, charged with erotic energy, as kissable as killable.) That's how the fight would arrive, and the men would battle to the edge of expulsion from the joint, if they were lucky and smart. Or the others, sensing that things were beginning to spin out of control, and feeling a holy holiday spirit, would stop coaxing them on and instead step in, saying: Break it up, guys. It was just Ron's fucking mistletoe. You don't want to get kicked out of here. And the two men would spit rage at each other and fight the hands that held them back until Ron, or whoever, would come into the room and they'd let go, turning away in disgust. That's how it would happen, Frankie thought, and then, after the meeting about following house rules, he'd have a chance to tell one of the stories he'd been holding, letting it flow out naturally, tapping into the post-fight vibe. Under those circumstances, he'd get it listened to in the right way. Just as Bernard, for his part—thin-lipped, bent-backed, haggard—might, on occasion, when the mood was right and he was up to it, launch into one of his rambling sermons, starting in on his time out west, drifting, looking for God in his own strange way. Just as Alex, who had a limited supply of stories so far, having gone around only once, might talk about a girl who took him to heaven and back by allowing him to snap the elastic edge of her panties while she held her hand along his spine, flat against it, just above his ass, resting it there quietly in anticipation.

·

I'd like to pause at this point. If I put Frankie's story in here, flashing forward, it would seem forced and ill-suited to the actual situation at hand, which included me at the top of the stairs, near the back door to Open Embrace, just beyond which lay the small office: a filing cabinet, a computer console, two desks—one for the man named Ron, the head of the joint, and one for the part-time social worker, Anne, who'd been there the last time I'd come to visit my brother, who was just settling in, jaunty with anxiety about getting along with the men, not sure what the deal was—he'd told me—with one of his roommates, a kid named Alex, who was about the same age as his own son, and who had his wife's name, to boot, making it all seem, as he'd said then, stranger than fiction. (You can't make that kind of shit up and get away with it, he'd told me. You'd be pushing the bounds and the bounds are what make the real world real and the fake bullshit fake, he'd said. He talked to me like that from time to time. The fact that he'd seen things I couldn't imagine, and I'd imagined things he couldn't see, allowed for an even balance between us. I loved him like a brother because he was my brother. But if you put that aside, there was a wide, angry, empty gap.) I was at the top of the stairs, looking down at the men, who were still facing the river and the trees, and still, as far as I could tell, perfectly silent. I could see the river—deep, dark—and the hills rising over Ossining. It was a beautiful vista, and it appeared to me, as I stood there, to betray the town of Haverstraw, which seemed crestfallen, with closed-up shop fronts and long streets that—when the light struck them properly, and you weren't looking closely—were just as desolate and sad and beautiful as anything Hopper painted. The townsfolk had the singular loneliness that he'd captured, standing apart from each other and gazing off into some distant future that would most likely never come. I'd written about the town before, in one form or another, and I knew that if I put too much of myself in the story it would become somewhat sentimental, because I found it hard to look upon a landscape without drawing a vestal sense, an obligation to hope that came not from the people—who, for the most part, had given up— but from the grandeur in the lovely fretwork that decorated the upper reaches of many of the houses, the sweeping front porches that seemed to be awaiting warm summer evenings and strollers with nothing to do but nod and call greetings. But there was more to it than that, of course, because the river itself, stretching beyond the men, beyond the trees, had no other choice but to represent the constant, eternal flow of time itself, and yet it was what it was and nothing else, just one more dogleg of the sea, its channel deep enough to let the salty tide slide up and back from day to day, running past the Battery, where, years ago, the towers fell and the dust rose and then, following the same pathway, drifted up past my brother and me as we stood in his yard smoking and talking and watching the kids. It seems to me that was the day my brother began his descent. But of course I'll never really know. It might just fit the mood. It might just be a good way of getting history into the story. The point is, I was at the top of the stairs looking down and could see beyond the trees to a part of the river the men couldn't see; and I knew that in a minute or two the quiet would end and my brother would turn and walk across the lot and stand before me, gaunt, sallow, but a bit stronger than the last time, and would speak of everything he'd lost in recent years—his wife, his house, his kids, his dog—and then I'd tell him to be careful not to compare his loss with others'. I'd offer that bit of advice, and then I'd mentally pry myself from him for a few seconds in an attempt to look upon his world from a wider vantage.

Five men smoking in a halfway house parking lot, four days before Christmas, twenty-five miles upstream from New York City, in a village that once ruled the brickmaking world.

THE MIGHTY SHANNON

The pain began in my hips, as far as I remember, and then moved to my lower back, and from there to my shoulders and then to my neck—while the shoulders continued to hurt. Then—and again, I'm doing my best to remember—it went back to my hips and, at the same time, struck my shoulders— this might've been a week or so later, and then it moved down to my heels while remaining in my hips, neck, and shoulders. Not my forefoot, where I've had pain before, or the plantar fascia, where I've had problems from running, but both heels, I said, and then I watched while Dr. Zuck, thin and limber-looking, most likely a runner himself, leaned forward again, ran his fingers along the film, and once again examined the X-ray of my neck. He'd heard it all before from me. We were starting to circle around a potential diagnosis. I'm sure we both felt it. He gave me a nod that said as much and put his finger to his chin. It was my third time in his office, and he had ordered blood work. He kept his finger on his chin and turned away, looking out the window as he spoke in a condescending voice and explained to me, again, that shadow pain migrating from one point to another might be indicative of any number of conditions, from fibromyalgia to Lyme disease—the latter admittedly unlikely given the two negatives on the Western blot, he said—to, well, certain types of cancer. Frankly, he said, cancer's also unlikely. But of course it is possible. As for a differential diagnosis, I'm not ready to make one yet, he said, and then he began to speak in general terms while his face stayed immobile, because he was the kind of doctor who struck deeply authoritative poses that kept dissolving to leave him looking absurdly young. Well, he said, we're starting to go around and around, which makes me inclined—granted, we need more blood work—to consider your stress levels, because it's very possible that some of this musculoskeletal pain, given everything we know so far, is related to your emotional life, he said, and then he instructed me to lie back on the table (I felt cold and vulnerable as I stood in my underwear before a floor-to-ceiling window while my own reflection—of course—came back at me: a blunt, broad-shouldered man pretending the best he could that he wasn't closing in on middle age while a barge navigated through his belly and the buildings of Fort Lee, New Jersey, stabbed through his breastbone). I lay back on the table while the doctor took a pin and pricked my toes (a faint itch), worked up to my heel (faint prick) and to my ankle (sharp, thorny prick), and then up my shin (jab). With each prick, he drew his breath through his nose and cleared his throat as if to speak, a little cluck of air coming from his mouth while the vents overhead hissed and through the glass came a single horn call from the tug pushing the barge—a familiar sound that transported me up the river to my house for a moment—and, when that died off, barely audible, the thrum of traffic on the West Side Highway and, pushing through it, the spongy, soft thump of my heart whiling away my life.

I did not want to acknowledge that one way or another my so-called migrating pain was connected to what was going on at home, not only with Sharon, who at that time was in the middle of her affair with a colleague at her firm, but also with my own thing with Marie, who was at that time my lover but also, in truth, a responsive gesture (as Dr. Haywood would later call it). I'm not sure, but I believe now that in Dr. Zuck's office, just after he pricked my shin, I was filled with fore-knowledge. This young doctor would not be able to nail down the cause of my pain, and I would go off to specialists at the Mayo Clinic—the beehive of clinical intensity inside while outside the thick summer heat glazed the Minnesota sky—and then the Cleveland Clinic, with all that corn-fed medical teamwork. I'm not saying that after each prick I knew a little bit more about what was coming, but lying there, wincing as he got beyond my shins, I was, I now think, aware that my physical condition, my pain, was prying my body from my mind.

Even there on that crinkling sheet of paper, with sweat beading on my brow, listening to Dr. Zuck breathe while the light outside faded and the light inside, fluorescent and shrill, pressed the glass, I had a sense that whatever was going on with my body was eventually going to find a way to relate itself to the extremely tactile facts of my life, my son, the house, the yard, as they, in turn, would relate to vague, nebulous, cloudy sensations that surrounded love, desire, loneliness, need. Then, as I stood (as instructed) on the cold tile and struggled to touch the floor, as Dr. Zuck stood back and watched, saying, Keep those knees straight, I felt exposed, small, fragile, like a core of chewy softness that had once been at the center of a hard shell, and for a second—with my hands yearning toward the floor—I became keenly aware of my predicament as it would unfold in the next few months, with bouts of intense pain and visits to figures of medical authority until, finally, the story of my pain—as Dr. Haywood would describe it—would merge with the story of my relationship with Sharon and our simultaneous assured destruction in the form of two affairs, although even now, years later, I have trouble apportioning blame equally between us because I'm still sure—from that tidy vantage of retrospect—that Sharon was the first to betray me, the first to stray off the map of our relationship, so to speak, and I was responding in kind, although I can admit—and I do admit!—that because I'm telling this from my vantage, the whole unseemly thing was ultimately on my shoulders.

•

Marie was the Spanish teacher at Gunner's school. Our thing began, I think, at a parent-teacher conference, as she leaned over her desk and spoke softly of Gunner's progress. He's a nice young man with an unusual gift for his age, an ability to be polite most of the time and to act as a mediator—she used the word *mediator*, I'm sure—when conflicts arise—she used the word *arise*—between other kids. A wonderful boy, she added, and then she gazed at me while her hair, flamboyantly curly, roiled around her face, which at that moment (I was feeling a fatherly sense of remove) looked beautifully young. Spread out on the desk, her hands, with long, professional fingers, were perfectly still. There wasn't a hint of flirtation or even erotic energy. That stayed, I now see, bound up in the building itself, the dull gray-blue cinder-block walls, the pale acoustic tile overhead, and the window behind her desk framing a view of the athletic field, chalked with lines, smothered in spring dusk. Nothing attracted us to each other, but then, a few weeks later, down at Hook Mountain State Park, I was sitting in my car reading the paper and smoking a cigar, and I called out to her as she passed, wrapped tight in jogging tights, her brow dappled with sweat, her hair pulled into a ponytail. She was still jogging slightly as she leaned down to exchange pleasantries. Hey, Miss Lorca. Hey, Gunner's dad. (Keenly aware of the code of public conduct between teacher and parent, I from that point avoided mention of Gunner.) Looking back, I think one thing that sparked our relationship was her awareness of my avoidance, and *my* awareness of *her* awareness, which fed a mutual effort to keep the two arenas separate, opening up a glorious no-man's-land, a pure space, unbinding and wild. I asked her about running and heard her say she was going to run a half marathon in Central Park. I offered her a tip on training. Do a few hills every other day, run backward uphill to strengthen your back, and then run forward downhill. Run wind sprints to get your legs used to going anaerobic when you kick it in at the finish. Don't go out too fast. You'll be inclined to push it hard and go with the crowd in the first mile, I might've said. But it's better to hold back, to be nuanced, to have a sense of what you can and can't do over the long haul, so check your splits during the first mile and resist the impulse to go with the flow—because for God's sake they'll be surging with an adrenaline flash and going out way too fast, beyond their capacities, except for the elite, and if you pace yourself you'll catch a lot of those who passed you initially, and they'll look like a bunch of stumbling fools, and you'll enjoy the hell out of it, I assure you. (Later I'd talk to her about carbo-loading and the way it felt to lead the Cleveland Marathon for a mile, far out ahead of the pack, feeling the terrible struggle of humanity behind me while a void opened in front of me, a pocket of silence—a windswept and pristine city street emptied of traffic for my own fucking sake, and my sake only—through which I plunged as if breaking the sound barrier. It's a feeling that never leaves you, I said. You carry it with you for the rest of your life. You long for it every minute of your existence, I think I said.)

She stopped jogging outside the car and put her forearm on the window. Her eyes seemed wet with concern, and seeing them I remembered that at the parent-teacher conference Sharon had been unusually polite to her, coolly reserved, and had held herself straight in the chair as if facing an adversarial presence. I now see that her taut-shouldered stance had been forming for weeks. In other words, the brisk way Sharon moved from teacher to teacher that night—taking our fifteen minutes, listening to positive and negative feedback, looking at test-score sheets—was a manifestation of her discomfort at being trapped with me in the evenings following afternoons in which she had walked with her lover hand in hand through the smell of spring as it mingled with the cool smell of the stone wall along the east side of Central Park. All this to say, when Marie leaned down and listened to my running advice, with her wonderful hair damp around her cheeks, I think she was responding not only to my words but also to the vibration of betrayal she had felt emanating from Sharon during the parent-teacher conference.

From that moment at Hook Mountain until the moment in the bedroom, in the postcoital quiet, with the tink of halyard coming across the water from the boat (mysterious in origin) that someone had moored twenty yards offshore, everything moved in a jaunty, quick way. Stories about classroom exploits—tales of the nose pickers and those with vomit breath, sweetie pies and bullies, kvetches and moralists, wide-eyed believers and cynics, towheads and freckle faces, snot noses and pencil eaters, the fainthearted and the lionhearted—joined the tattoo above her belly button, her orgasmic yelp, the tuck of her ass, her landlocked gaze, our paired singsong cries, the painful and the pleasurable grunts, and the weird warp of time (no other way to describe it) I got when she sneaked over during her lunch breaks—extended by a fifth-period planning slot—and stood in the doorway knocking (an endearing formality, why shouldn't I admit it?), waiting as I stood inside and scanned the street for anyone who might happen to be passing. Everything seemed to squeeze into that bright instant before she crossed the threshold into the house. Behind her, the trees across the street heaved into the heat. Inside my house, I felt not only the guilt and fear you'd expect but also the same brooding sense of myself I'd get two years later at our annual holiday cocktail party, standing at the window and looking out at the cold, wintry street while behind me someone shook a shaker with an icy sound, like a comet flying through the din of chat, and I stared outside for a few beats beyond civility and felt, behind me, the party I was hosting awaiting my return. One more man staring out his window, feeling the weight of his obligations shove him into a loneliness that was almost, but not quite, beyond comprehension. To push further: When I was a wee—yes, wee—boy of about nine, I stood in the upstairs bedroom window of Grandfather's house, in Michigan, with my nose pressed to the glass, looking out at the wintry street, and had the exact same sensation in a more youthful form as I heard, rising up through the hardwood floor and then through the gray wool carpeting, the murmur of a bridge game being played in the front parlor (as Grandma called it) on folding tables, and I felt completely separated from earthly reality while at the same time erotically entwined in it. To push further: I would feel this sensation when, on a kind of second honeymoon trip to Ireland, at Mizen Head, on the edge of the continent, as close to the United States as we could get, with the wind whipping Fastnet lighthouse, a small stub of human ingenuity on a spit of rock in a raging sea behind us, Sharon and I embraced and held each other as if in grief, and my eye went out over the water to someplace far, far beyond, and I felt our solitude and companionship combined for just a few seconds while, at the same time, Sharon's hair, smelling sweet from the shampoo she'd bought in Paris, tangled around my lips. To push further: Years later, with Gunner grown up and off on his own, when we were back in Ireland for what I guess you might call our third honeymoon (but also to visit Sharon's mother in Tralee), at a place called Carrick-on-Shannon, we walked into town from the train station after the trip from Dublin. The weather warm and sunny, Sharon and I were happy to be moving again, rolling the suitcases along the sidewalk. The mighty, mighty Shannon, one of us said as we came to the bridge and to the river itself, not small but not large, either, by Hudson River standards. We sat and looked at the river while on the bank racing sculls dried in the sun, and the pock of a tennis ball came from a public court, and the narrow river sluiced, clean and glossy, out of the cold, ancient arch of the bridge, and then, right then, we began—because we were both thinking about the same thing—to laugh, both of us, her soft flutter and then my own throat throwing out a laugh in return, until we were in hysterics. Here you are, the laugh seemed to be saying, with the years behind you, the years gone, after all that child rearing, after your own fuckups, sharing a laugh together in a country where the collective survival tactic is to twist pain into language, to make a joke over a pint of Guinness with an edge that comes from having no other recourse but to take a brute reality—famine and subjugation to distant authority—and turn it into a punch line that seems to be, but really isn't, at the expense of your own national identity.

·

In the doorway with Marie that afternoon—this was in the middle of July, with sunny days succeeding one another, the grass brown, the river low, with a band of tidal wash exposed on the wall at the end of the yard—before she crossed the threshold into my arms, I had a premonition. I'm not saying I saw over the edge of time in a prophetic sense or anything like that, but I'm pretty sure I knew what was coming as I felt the twinge in my neck, or the tweak in my hip, or maybe the electrical tingle I got along the undersides of my wrists. By that point, I had a suspicion that Sharon was having an affair, a suspicion sparked by a single incident. (No hair clips in the bathroom, no hairs on the pillow, no smell of unusual cologne on her dresses, no weird physical tension—although she had seemed distant that summer, and more of our conversations had had to do, in one way or another, with Gunner. We'd found a way of draping everything with his needs: the fury of our parenting patter like the indeterminate cloud of electrons orbiting a nucleus, a shell created out of our frantic concerns.

Often our concern was that we were being too concerned and that we'd somehow interfere with some natural physics. At all costs we wanted to avoid instructing from above, or hovering, or helicoptering.) One afternoon, my cell phone began to twitter and Sharon's name came up on the screen and I heard, when I answered, the distinct tonality of a pocket dial, an accidental portal. I felt, as I stood in the back room and looked out at the water with the phone to my ear, my face in her purse, tucked against her wallet. I could smell the leather and feel the intricate arabesque tooling. I could feel it brush against my ear. There was the far-off throb of a man's voice, and a muffled exchange—along with the sound of footsteps—and I was sure that she was walking with someone in Manhattan. The air was charged with the clicking heels of commerce and noontime release. (Later I'd imagine they were strolling near his apartment, at Eighty-First and Lexington, or along Central Park, or sitting together on the top step at the entrance to the Metropolitan Museum of Art, holding hands, enjoying the conversation, totally unsuspecting that I was, thirty miles upstream, inside her purse, listening.) On the phone I heard banter, a bump of voices—I think—and then, suddenly a burst of sound, bright and pure and sustained, arriving in a digitized sizzle. It was her highest and most delighted utterance. I knew it, hearing it, right off. It was the giggle she made—and I knew this, I swear—only in response to something said in the most intimate terms. I stood and listened until it died away, and then, finally, overcome with a sense of helplessness, I shouted: Hey, hey, I'm here in your purse, Sharon. I'm right here. I'm in your fucking purse. Even now, years later, I'm ashamed of having been privy to a moment in her life from that vantage. It was as if I'd gone behind her face for a moment and stared out through the bright blood spume of her eyelids.

Much, much later I would combine the shame I felt hearing the pocket dial, which came from the fact that a link had been unintentionally opened up between my world at the window, looking out at the river, and Sharon's world somewhere on the East Side, walking and talking with someone, with the shame I felt when she told me that she often went for walks with him during lunch down Madison all the way to the Flatiron Building, and then up Fifth Avenue as far as time allowed, and that it had been during those walks that the banter and office talk had deepened, becoming serious, intimate and loving, an exchange of private information, while between the words, between the phrases and the confessions, a void had opened up into which love rushed. (At least that's the way I see it.) As I imagine it, they felt that clandestine sense of New York isolation as they walked down Madison, following the slight decline—a hill, a Manhattan hill!—keeping their eyes as far ahead as possible over the bob of heads. Lovers look far ahead to the end of the landscape as they hold hands, I suppose. Lovers fix their gazes as if to approximate a location for the heart. The violet, arboreal haze from the park. The sidewalk luring itself toward the museum. Again, the smell of the park commingling with the wet of the wall and the warm smell from the pavement. Later, I'd imagine them going down the stairs into a restaurant for lunch, down a short flight of concrete stairs, holding a wrought-iron handrail. A little French bistro, ready-made for secret lunches. I'd imagine them steeped in that wonderful incognito sense of being together below street level, with the murmur of table talk around them. I'd never really know, but I'm sure he was the sort of fastidious guy who dabbed daintily at his chin or upper lip with his napkin. Dabbed absently, obsessively—a habit attached to a shadow memory of a long-gone college mustache. I imagined he was tall and formal, with a narrow chin and big, greenstone eyes. He had an old-school dignity and wore suits tailored snug around his shoulders so that when he shifted, which he rarely did, there was a starchy rustle from his shirts. All I really knew about him, all I would ever know, was that he was an upstanding, deeply thoughtful soul who somehow—at that particular time, under those particular conditions—had wooed my wife, who in turn had wooed him, and for a few months they had puzzled together something that resembled love, although she'd later tell me, again and again and again and again, that it really wasn't love but rather a lonely lust born of, of, well, you know what, she said, because I had also explained to her that Marie wasn't an object of my love (although she was) and was simply a stand-in for an idea of something I couldn't pin down except to say—and I did say, again and again and again—that it embodied itself in her sweet response to my pain. (She was lonely, I was lonely. What else can I say? I hurt, she soothed. We were mutually consumed in a mutual loneliness, I said, I think.) Even now, when I try to imagine him, I see his fingers, nimble and thin, with downy brown hair on the knuckles, gently pinching his napkin into a point and padding it softly along his lip. I see a flat-footed dignity, spit-shined shoes, and a Chicago-born (because he was from Chicago) sense of exchange value based on the relationship between the hinterlands and the city. I still imagine a prairie wind ruffling his razor-cut hair to reveal his scalp. I can see her reaching up and ruffling his hair the way she had so often ruffled Gunner's hair. In the same way, I imagine that *she* imagines Marie tending to me after the fit of pain struck—and it did strike—before or after one of our own trysts. I imagined, and *still* imagine, that she imagined, and still imagines,

Marie, with her brown skin and her long fingers and her
teacherly attention, gently touching the places I told her hurt
me, or putting her hand flat between my shoulder blades and
rubbing vigorously, as instructed. I imagined that Sharon
imagined, and still does imagine, a woman with a slight accent quoting García Lorca, saying, "*No duerme nadie por el
cielo. Nadie, nadie,*" while she stood in her panties at the window and sunlight bathed her hips, knowing that I was looking
at her and getting, standing there, that sense of self-awareness
that fed itself back from my looking to her knowing.

•

In the doorway that afternoon—with Marie pausing ceremo-
nially on the other side of the threshold, waiting a few seconds
for me to formally beckon her inside, sustaining the tension
for the fucking pleasure of it in her yellow dress, her shoulders exposed, a dapple of freckles—I shook the tingle from my
hands and waved her in, casting a glance outside to make sure
all was clear, and it was, only the hiss of cicadas, and the street,
beyond the driveway, empty and quiet. The outside world was
quiet and the inside world was quiet and there was, before I
closed the door, as we stood together in the vestibule, a moment
similar to the abovementioned moments with Sharon. I remember how, just before the door closed, the summer light
became a small sliver that seemed to struggle against the rubber seal and then was gone, sucked away, and it was just the
two of us, standing in the air-conditioned air, our feet shush-
ing on the cold tiles in the vestibule as we moved against each
other and the tingle in my hands migrated to my elbows and
then to my shoulder blades, foreshadowing what was to come:
It would hit again, as it had the other times. Then she'd tend

to me and I'd respond, saying, higher, lower, spread your hand out and use the flat of your palm, more to the left, a little bit more to the left, right there, right there, right there, perfect. And even if the pain continued—and it always did—I'd give a long moan and make a show of feeling better, straightening up, pulling on my pants. Then I'd offer her a cup of coffee or tea and we'd sit in the kitchen or on the back patio relaxing while she spoke lovingly and with joy about her students and I imagined her moving around seductively in the smell of chalk dust, the polished floors beneath her heels, the clunk of chairs. Then she'd say she had to go, and she'd kiss me and be on her way.

On the penultimate day, as I now think of it, the point through which the rest of my life with Sharon would seem to bow, or, rather, bend, so that everything that transpired after that afternoon seemed to lead to the day when Sharon confessed to me, admitted that, yes, she had been seeing X, but that she had broken it off with him, let go of him, was how she put it—on that day, Marie sat in the wrought-iron chair on the patio, leaning down into a compact mirror and applying lipstick as she spoke, saying, Look, I'm not the nursemaid type. The truth is I just don't think I'm up to the task. And I said, But you're good, you're really good. You're making me feel better. If it helps, I won't talk about the pain. I'll keep it to myself, I said. And she snapped the compact shut and looked up at me and said, I'm not a nurse. It's not in my blood. It was in my mother's blood until she met my father. When she met my father she was a nurse in a small town called Carboneras. She worked for the only doctor in town until my father turned her into a full-blown nurse, if you know what I mean. And I told her, I don't know what you mean. And she explained to me that certain men are in need of constant care. I'm not that woman to give that kind of care, she said. Then she went on to explain that her father had been injured in a fishing accident off the coast of Almería. Something about a winch, some rope, his fingers, and a dislocated shoulder. I went to the edge of the patio and stood looking out while behind me, over the hill, the dog days of summer approached. Was it that bad? I said, and she said, Well. Yes. Yes, it was that bad. (Often I'd complain of some pain as a way of getting her touch, guiding her hand to certain places, but on that day in July, as we had released each other, sweating slightly, my back had tightened and a second later, as I swung my legs and began to lift myself up, my body had been lassoed by spasm. I had gone through the motions of standing up, stretching, making a swimming motion with my hands, fending the pain off as much as I could, saying, It was just a tweak, just a little tweak, and she had said, If that's a tweak I'd like to see a twinge.)

A few minutes later I walked her to the front door and took a peek outside to make sure the coast was clear. Nothing but the trees across the street casting pools of shade. Nothing but a quiet street. Inside, with the door open, we hugged each other one last time, and then I watched as she walked quickly down the sidewalk. The cold air rushed past me as it streamed out of the house. There is a complicit, accusatory nature to this day, I think I thought, watching her leave, and it seems to me now that the way the trees suddenly quivered and shifted, and the way, a few minutes later, when I was in the kitchen with a cup of coffee, popping an oxycodone, thinking about the upcoming appointment with Dr. Zuck, trying to recall the exact path the pain had taken, the sky darkened and the surface of the river—which I can now admit I spent obsessive amounts of time observing—became stucco with wind; something in all that told me Sharon and I would end up in an office on Madison Avenue (and we did) with some shrink, most likely a surprisingly young woman with the habit of tweezing her earlobe while she listened to me explain that it was the physical pain that led me into the situation with Marie. The pain was in need of a nurse, of a certain kind of touch, I'd explain (and I did). She was good with the pain, I imagined I might say, and I did say. And Sharon would say, and did say, You're full of shit. No woman could stand your complaining. You moaned and belly-ached from the beginning. I remember your twisted ankle when we lived on Greenwich Street. Your bum knee on Claremont Avenue. Your ankle at Rockefeller rink. Your hamstring in Michigan. Not to mention your hip—I think it was a stress fracture—in Vermont. I won't even go into that. You've always verbalized every single fucking pain, no matter how minor. I mean for God's sake, you never drew a line, she would say, I imagined, and she *did* say. And I'd say, and I did say: I'm not claiming that what Dr. Zuck is now calling migrating inflammation points were a direct response to your betrayal of our wedding vows. That's speculation on my part, although it makes perfectly good sense. I'd argue—and I'm going to stick with this defense for the rest of my life—that one reason I began the thing with Marie, one huge factor, was the way she was sympathetic without being judgmental. I mean she really seemed to care, I'd say, and I did. She was an epic nursemaid. She even said once, and I'll quote: I'm what you'd call a nursemaid type. I'm a teacher, sure, but I'm also a hell of a good nurse. End quote. Then in the shrink's office there would be, and there *was*, a dull, subdued pause. That's bullshit, Sharon would say, and did say. That's pure bullshit. No woman would tolerate your bitching and moaning in the early stages of a relationship—even a fling. You didn't tell her about the pain because you didn't have the pain until long after you started fucking her, she said, as Dr. Haywood raised her palm flat in the air, as if pushing against something, and adjusted her hair and tossed her head slightly in what seemed to me, again, an unprofessional way, and then, from that point, began to explain her theory of establishing a safe zone between our two arguments, a kind of no-man's-land from which we could each wave a white flag. Her voice rose and fell as it tried to establish an intimate formality, working hard to sound responsive to our specific situation. She told us that Gunner had to be considered first, and that whatever we did or said, no matter what happened, we'd have to make sure that we kept him front and center. We'd have to create a safe zone where we could wave white flags at each other. That's about all I can remember. White-flag waving. No-man's-land. A safe zone. Putting Gunner first. And the way a tissue came out of the box on her desk, a single O'Keeffeian bloom, pure and bright.

•

Jesus, Dr. Haywood and her safe zone and white-flag waving, I said to Sharon, months after that session, sitting out on the back deck, talking quietly with drinks in hand. Night was falling. It was midsummer and there was a slight briny smell in the air. The yard was dark. We sat for a few minutes, holding hands across the table in an anticipatory quiet that came from years of being together, half knowing what the other might say, half not knowing. I would talk a little more about Dr. Haywood's fluty, high-strung voice, and the way she held her hand up like a referee when she wanted us to stop shouting. Then we began to laugh together, softly at first. A light, summer-evening laugh. (To push further: If you were hiding in the bushes on the north side of the yard, or behind one of the pines, or even deep in the Thompsons' yard, you'd hear the hugely intimate, forgiving sound of it as it started in Sharon's throat, a series of thin, brittle wheezes, and then my response, a single bark, and then in response her fluttery laugh combined, a half second later, with my own weird *he ha, he ha*, until we fed each other into an entwined sound that was very likely—although I'm certainly pushing too far here—like a Bach counterpoint: two themes working together in a helix of motion, twisting around a dark heavenly void that might be where God, if he lives, lives. Hearing it, you'd be able to tease out the story that had produced the laugh, because we were both remembering the way I had fallen to the floor of Dr. Haywood's office, the pain in my back striking unusually fast, so that I ended up pumping my legs, trying to ease it, and then—you'd almost be able to get this, listening—the way I refused assistance, saying, I'm perfectly fine, nothing hurts at all, I don't feel a thing, and I stumbled out of the office, through the sound of the two white-noise machines, down the stairs, and onto Park Avenue. If you listened with enough sensitivity, you'd hear in our laughter the way Sharon had caught up with me near Grand Central and scooped me from behind in what would, much later, seem to me the first hints of a playfulness that is, if you're lucky, the wonderful byproduct of forgiveness.)

INSTRUCTIONS FOR A FUNERAL

Dear Morrison: As instructed, I've put down a few thoughts about a memorial service. I'll have this notarized later in the morning. The house is quiet. The river is catching dawn light. I've been up all night.

•

As the mourners arrive, play Glenn Gould's version of the Bach French Suite no. 2 at a volume loud enough to mask the shuffling of feet and the scraping of chairs and, if it happens to be spring, the sound of birds outside; if it's early fall and windows are open, the dead-leaf rustle.

Include a note in program: "On good days William Kenner felt the glory of existence in the phrasing, in the arched fingers striking the keys. He spent way too much time imagining Gould on the shore of the lake, hands deep into his pockets, head bent forward, with the Canadian sky looming over him. He spent too much time trying to connect Gould's so-called idea of north with his own Michigan idea of north: those sudden midsummer chills that hit Petoskey, and that one night in particular when the pine cones froze off the trees and drummed on the tin porch roof outside his bedroom window."

When everyone's seated, play "Like a Rolling Stone." Note in the program: "When alive, Kenner spent too much time pondering Dylan's lyrics and never did figure out who that mystery tramp might've been, although he did often like to think that the figure came out of the hinterlands, one more American sociopath, perhaps, and he knew the type from his own boyhood, having seen them come and go, taking his sister out at night, pulling up at the curb in the summer haze of the streetlamp." Everyone should remain seated during this music portion of the program, including Don Philpot, who, if he's still alive, will be nervously pinching the flesh on his upper lip where, as a teenager, he had a mustache. He'll be fidgeting because—I like to imagine—he'll be thinking about the Newburgh deal. He might also be thinking about the time the four of us went down to the Amish quilt auction in Lancaster, Pennsylvania, and we got into an argument about the motions of the spotters. Philpot maintained that the men doing the signaling were intuitively manipulating the invisible field of energy—those are his words exactly—that formed around any kind of interaction that might lead to a deal. If you were keen enough, he claimed, you could tweak this field to your own advantage in the bidding.

Next, play the original versions of Louis Armstrong's "West End Blues" and then "St. James Infirmary" (six minutes thirty-one seconds total), at which point—presumably—Philpot will break into one of his sweating fits, wiping his forehead with his handkerchief, adjusting his ass on the seat, sulky with shame.

Please note in the program the following: "Kenner sat on

the board of the New York State Real Estate Ethics Committee and chaired the Committee for Real Improvement in Real
Estate. He worked tirelessly for justice." On the other hand,
if it's clear that I was killed by Sullivan, please substitute the
following: "Kenner tangled with the Evil. Gangster. Sullivan,
who, in concert with a dear friend, shafted him out of the land
in Newburgh and proceeded to build the Highland Estates,
yet another bedroom community of commuters who had to
cross the bridge to catch the train in Beacon when, if I'd had
my way, they might've taken the ferry that Kenner (I) was well
on the way to putting into service, having already, at the time of
the bid, through careful nursing of connections to the state,
received all the permits and pilot certificates necessary to
develop a high-speed Newburgh/Manhattan service." I pondered way too much not only the bedroom community that
Philpot built, the cluster of nondescript buildings, the terraces
with unusually low railings (the jerk had the Newburgh building inspector in his pocket too), but also the lives of those
who lived in the units and commuted to Manhattan from upstate every day, rising at dawn, dressing quietly in the dark so
as not to wake their wives, or husbands, and then slogging
across the miserable bridge to the train and the long ride down
to the city, and then, hours later, returning home in the dark—
except in the summer, when the glorious Hudson Valley,
bathed in warm dusk, would mock their servitude; whereas
I, through financial finesse and my intuitive sense of the volume needed to project my ideas past the scratchy noise of the
real estate market, had found a way to spare the commuters
such a fate. Just as Louis Armstrong, with his ability to play
loudly and in tune at the same time, was able to project through
the limitations of the Victrola and then, later, of mono AM

radio filled with static. His horn threw itself in front of the background noise, doing whatever it wanted to do, joyful and strong.

When the Armstrong piece is over, please ask for a moment of silence. If Philpot is still alive and in attendance—with sweat beading on his brow and his long legs jittering—he'll find this short pause unendurable, and he'll sense that Armstrong is mocking his inability to play the market honestly.

Note: I would like my body to be on display, dressed in a clean white shirt, black tie, dark trousers, along with my hand-sewn Italian shoes. (Please have them resoled.) I'd like the undertaker to clean up the razor-burn blemishes under my chin and trim my eyebrows and my ear and nose hairs. Please tilt the coffin slightly toward the room so that a view of my body is unavoidable. If my face is disfigured by an act of violence—most likely at the hands of Sullivan, but possibly Bob Hartwell, who had a grudge against me because of the tree-chopping incident, the border dispute, and the subsequent surveying expenses, and who stopped acting in a neighborly fashion around 1991—do your best to clean up the blemishes on my neck and the small crater on my left eyelid, which still bothers me because I remember the cauterizing tool the dermatologist used, the unexpected burst of pain, and the smell of flesh burning. Again, even if my face is a Cubist mess, please present it to the mourners. Please put a note in the program, or make an announcement after the moment of silence:

"It was William Kenner's wish that each of you take one last look at his face. Please make every attempt humanly possible to take at least one glance. Even if his face fills you with the sharp envy (you, Philpot!) of knowing that he'd had the

Archdiocese of New York in the palm of his hand when he ne-
gotiated the easement for the entry road to the retirement
home for nuns, which later became fondly known around
town as the Nunnery. Kenner often admired the meadow
property—beautiful as the grass swayed in the wind off the
river, only thirty miles north of Manhattan. Kenner had
bought the meadow long before he moved to town. He and
Ann rented a car and drove out of the city in search of a
country house, a weekend retreat, and when they came to the
meadow, with the palisade looming over the northern border,
they got out of the car, waded into the grass, and fucked each
other senseless. Then, on the way out, Kenner spotted the
FOR SALE sign and bought the land that would, years later,
retrospectively, even a score."

One afternoon, over lunch, we declared ourselves business partners of the old-school type, willing to seal deals
with a handshake and a smile. Why bother signing a contract
when friendship and trust would suffice? You may recall, Don
(my corpse might say), that Ann and I made a number of over-
tures of friendship to you and Marie. One was the invitation
to join us for our annual trip to the Amish auction near Lancaster. These were, you'll recall, the days when we were keeping a tally of our dinner-party invites. We owed you an invite
equivalent to three of your parties, and I figured that even with
your petty accounting you'd see a trip to Amish country at our
expense as the equivalent to eating Marie's food three times.
I figured, and Ann did, too, that you understood that we at-
tended your dinner parties out of compassion.

Note to Morrison, if you're still alive and still my counsel
when you get this document, or to Comstock, or Swinburne,
if you take over as my counsel, or to whoever at Morrison,

Comstock & Swinburne happens to land the job of tending to this document, here are a few key points:

- After the tidal flood, the terraces' collapse, and subsequent lawsuits, Don's betrayal of me with Sullivan's help probably cost him a shitload of legal fees.

- Again, in retrospect, the score between us was already even, because long before the Newburgh deal I'd fleeced the archdiocese, and therefore Rome and indirectly Philpot's supposedly devoted wife (she wasn't), who—as Don told me one evening as we hiked together to the top of Hook Mountain— Oz-like, majestic—saw herself as a vassal of Rome and, through Rome, of the Holy Spirit. In other words, by dickering with the archdiocese, which was determined to build the home for the nuns on that property, I was actually dickering with Don's wife, who tithed a percentage of his income to the Church and thus, via the Church and the meadow deal, to me.

- I simply did what any self-respecting business-man might have done if he'd had the good fortune of owning the sliver of land that the Church needed to house retired nuns in dignity and safety, with a beautiful view. I didn't buy the meadowland intending to exploit it.

- In death I'll feel absolved of guilt and yet still sorrowful about the rending of a friendship.

- I intend, if I'm not killed by Sullivan, or in a freak accident of some kind, to continue telling my son the story of Philpot's betrayal as a lesson in how deep trust and friendship can be exploited for material gain. I intend to sit him down again and say, "Son, I don't know if you remember my old friend, Don Philpot, who used to come over to the house when you were a boy." My hope is to wait until I'm on my deathbed to tell him the story again, making use of the deathbed aura, the beep of the machine as a backbeat. I'll explain that our friendship went back to my childhood in Michigan, before I moved out here, and I'll tell my son about the time when Don and I were slapping a puck around on Portage Pond, and on a dare he skated as close as he could to the inlet where the creek went under the road. He fell through the pale blue ice, and I shimmied on my belly with my stick, spreading my legs to disperse the weight as I guided him to shore. Then I took off his wet clothes, wrapped him in my coat, and took him to my car, where I cradled and hugged him to warm him. I saved his life. He said as much over the years. He said, I owe you my life, Kenner. He said it over lunch that day. He said, That time you were playing around with that kid, Brent, in the rail yard, you saved his foot, and then a few months later, you saved my life. Not bad. Most of us would be satisfied with saving one foot, or a life, but to save a foot and a life is a big, big thing, he said. And I said, Don, it was nothing. All I did was help you slide along the ice to the shore, and it wasn't that far. I'll tell my son that he

thanked me again and again over the years for saving his ass. His ass, I'll tell my son. He told me I
saved his ass. But the way I think about it, I saved
an ass. I'll stress that it's dangerous to do business
with an old friend. Precise memory vaporizes when
it comes into contact with cash. (Morrison: It's possible that by the time these instructions get put into
action I'll have already told the story again to an
older version of my son, so it's possible that my son
will be giving Philpot the evil eye during the moment of silence. If you're alive and attending, please
watch him. If he gives Don the evil eye, you can
safely assume that he's heard the lifesaving/ice story
as it relates to the Newburgh/betrayal story. If not,
you can assume that I didn't have a chance to tell
it to him again because I died at the hand of Sullivan,
who, I might as well add here, called me the other
night, I think. Someone called with a thick accent,
or with a handkerchief over the mouthpiece [do
they still do that?] and spoke in a mumbled tone
about vindication.)

• I tried—and I'm still trying—to instill in my son a
sense of compassion strong enough to develop into
an ethos of love, so that he'll eventually be able to
find it in himself to forgive a heinous, albeit typically
American, act of financial violence, along with a betrayal of a handshake: an extended squeeze of flesh
on flesh and a big up-and-down shake that lasted for
about a minute as we chuckled and agreed that we
were the best of friends and that no written contract

was necessary. A sense of shared destiny threw us back to the Midwest, and I mentioned this to Philpot after the shake. I said: Isn't it amazing that two fuck-up kids from the sticks are closing a friendly handshake deal for what might be the largest land grab north of Bear Mountain in years?

- As an example of extreme forgiveness, I told my son the story of Bill Burdick, who opened fire on a Pizza King. I painted a complete picture: gray sky over an upstate town. Diners eating pizza, folding food into their mouths. You have to see it, I told my son, who was only ten at the time. Imagine ten people sitting at tables with red and white checks, a red candle at each, I said. Five days before Christmas, mind you. A postcard tableau, a warm port in the storm of a recession, with most of the storefronts outside boarded and a few other buildings gutted by arson fires. Everything cozy inside, with a jukebox playing Louis Armstrong's original version of "What a Wonderful World." Eating pizza, they were oblivious to the misfortune walking down the street. But that pizza parlor, for whatever reason, was waiting for Burdick. (My son looked bored. He rolled his eyes.) Just as the patch of land I purchased years back, the so-called meadowland up the road, you know, the meadow where we go sometimes to walk, was begging to be denuded and graded in preparation for digging; you smooth and grade first and then you dig out the hole, line it with plywood, and pour a foundation. (I'll retell the Burdick story again when he's older. You forget most of what you hear at age ten. You get the rudiments and then let the rest float away. If I don't live, he'll still have the basic gist of the Burdick story to instruct him on compassion and forgiveness.) I unfolded—and might do so again in the near future, if I live—the pizza-parlor scene in order to prepare him for one of the main points, which was that Burdick had admitted that he massacred the pizza parlor "for the hell of it because it was waiting for me to do it," he said, first in the initial police interrogation and then, later, in front of the packed courtroom. Burdick took the stand *against the advice of counsel* and explained, simply, that he'd killed fifteen folks "for the hell of it."

(Morrison: Do you remember the conversation we had a few years ago, in which you explained to me that one out of every twenty or so clients could be counted on to go against your counsel? You said: "It's often the most judicious souls, the considerate ones who go against the advice of counsel." Then, in another meeting, you told me: "It is counsel's advice that you keep your mouth shut about Sullivan. Let it go. Do not attempt to approach Sullivan. Don't make public or even private statements about Newburgh, Sullivan, or Philpot.")

- The other point of the Burdick story was that the sole survivor of the Pizza King massacre, LeAnne Kelly, whose St. Christopher medallion necklace

deflected a kill shot to the chest, had offered forgiveness to Burdick. "If Burdick could attempt to
kill me for the hell of it, then I have every right to
forgive him for the hell of it," she said in a television
interview. She had big hazel eyes and a long, elegant
nose. She spoke with composure, pursing her lips
slightly, pursing them some more, and then re-
leasing her mouth into a gorgeous smile. I wasn't
saved from the financial bullet of betrayal, I'll say
to my son, or will have said: No such luck for your
old man. I didn't have a St. Christopher medal
around my neck, so to speak, to spare me betrayal
by an old friend.

As for the eulogy and all of that, I think I'll leave most of
it to the living (whoever they might be) to plan that part of the
service, although let me say for the record that I'd like the
Reverend Woo, if he's still around, to give one of his long-
winded, incomprehensible sermons, drawing from the book
of Job and whatever passage he can find that contains the word
vainglory—something from Philippians, perhaps. Note: Please
ask Woo to pound on the word *vainglory*. And then I assume
that there will be the usual personal comments from grieving
family members and then, if I live long enough, perhaps my
son, perhaps a young man by now, might get up and tell the
story of my taking the train down to Yonkers to find Sullivan,
one clear winter day (yesterday, to be precise), and going to
his so-called social club, a ratty little building with windows
covered with faded newsprint. I'd seen the building many
times on the news, during coverage of the so-called Boss
War, in the summer of 1987, when Sullivan was supposedly

solidifying control of the Eastern Syndicate, as they kept calling it. On television, it was a classic brick storefront with an old sign—Hudson Shoe Repair—with missing neon tubes. When I saw it in person, it looked astonishingly shabby, a stubby brick building in a block of high-rises and condos not far from the railroad station. In person, it seemed to radiate a criminal desperation. Just seeing it, from across the street, filled me with confidence. The Sullivan gang—according to reports—was now fragmented and losing power by the day. I like to imagine that my son will use this story to illustrate my gumption, my fearlessness. The truth is, I *felt* fearless. Fueled by my anger and my almost cosmic sense of betrayal (You, Don! You miserable liar. Judas. Handshake deceiver), I marched right up to the door, gave it a knuckle rap, and waited for an eye to appear in the eyehole. Someone on the other side of the door grunted a phrase. I knocked again and heard the grunt again. Password, the grunt seemed to be saying, and I said, I don't know the password. I'm here to speak to Sullivan. He doesn't know it, but he's expecting me. When the door opened, I was facing an old man with a cane. He was toothless, with one eyelid stuck shut. He kept one hand clutched behind the lapel of his tweed jacket, looked me up and down with his good eye, and said, What do you want? I said, I've come in search of the truth about a matter. And he said, What matter? And I said, It's an upstate matter. (Let me stress here that I had an intuitive sense of how to speak.) Upstate how? he said. And I said, Upstate land. Stay here, he said, and he closed the door and left me standing outside in the fresh air, with the blue sky overhead. I stood and stood and felt my feet on the ground.

I felt like a man ready to defend his honor. I felt like a man ready to defend his honor against the forces of evil, so to speak. I felt like a man standing outside an old shoe-repair shop in the Yonkers business district, with the sound of the Metro-North train arriving at the station a few blocks away, trailing a long strand of tension and stress as it tried to brake to a stop; and then, a minute later, the repowering, the gathering steam. It was an express, I knew, because expresses were diesel-powered so they could pass Croton, where the third rail ended, and head all the way up past Beacon to the end of the line in Poughkeepsie. The sound of the train leaving filled me with strength—I'll explain to my son. A minute later, the door opened and the man appeared again and gestured me with a wave of his cane into a dark room that smelled of shoe polish and cleaning compounds and gun oil. There were a few old tables and even older chairs. The man led me to the back, lifted a gate, and pushed me behind a counter where, in a reclining chair, Sullivan sat with a cigar in his mouth, a friendly look on his face. (If I'm dead now, Morrison, please know that it has something to do with the feeling I got when I saw his face, because it seemed to me, as he gestured toward a chair, that he had honest eyes, deep twinkling blue. It's also possible—if I'm dead now and you're reading this a few weeks later—that I was fooled by his casual voice as he said, Go ahead, state your business. Tell me who you are and what you want. It was a fatherly voice.) I dove right in and told him everything from my point of view. I told him about Philpot (you, Don!) and our early friendship, the time I saved his life on the ice in Michigan, and then about the handshake deal and the Newburgh land and our agreement to use state funds to finance a high-speed ferry service to the city. As I spoke, he listened attentively and swung his cigar in the air, making short looping gestures, as if conducting. Again, his eyes seemed to twinkle as I spoke of the bond I'd felt with Philpot, one that came from sharing hour after hour of our boyhood days. We were further bonded, I explained to Sullivan, by our both having abandoned Michigan for the East Coast. As he listened, Sullivan's eyes seemed to tear up. (Up until this point, I now see, I had not gone against your counsel, Morrison. I was simply a confessor bemoaning a business deal gone sour.) I was nothing but a lonely man in Yonkers, on a clear, beautiful winter day, spilling his soul to a man who was notoriously quick-tempered; who had killed, according to news accounts, at least a hundred men. He seemed, as he swung his hand, trailing smoke, to understand my honor as it related to risk and death, and I'm sure now, as I write this (it's late and I've been drinking), that he understood, up to a point, my willingness to go against common sense. I'd even say that he seemed impressed with me as he said, Go on. I get it. Go on. You left the homeland for the East. So I did go on. I accused Philpot (you, Don!) of conspiring with him against me on the silent bid for the Newburgh land. I implied, against the advice of counsel, that the two of them had been in cahoots against me, and that someone would have to pay for the crime, somehow.

If I tell this story to my son, I'll stop right here, pull up short and avoid describing being led out of the social club after shaking Sullivan's hand. I'll say I got confirmation that Philpot had truly fucked me. I'll keep it clean and simple. I'll avoid telling my son about the way Sullivan's face changed, about the way his eyes became dead cold, blurry blue, and his lips became firm and tight against his teeth in a smile that seemed politely politic, charged with a task of hiding a placid, benign malice toward his audience. (As a matter of fact, Sullivan looked a bit like old photos of JFK. Beautifully haunted as he looked out at the world with a gentility and authority tempered with physical pain.) I'll avoid telling my son about the way Sullivan's attention went from me to his cigar, which he examined carefully, and then, after clearing his throat a few times, he began to speak in a voice that was tight and intense. He told me about his best friend, years back, in Hell's Kitchen (back when *hell* was still in the *kitchen*, he said), a kid named Kenny Bruen, and how they worked together, pickpocket schemes on the subway, this and that, until they were both working for what he called a higher establishment. Then one day the fork appeared, he said. The big fork that always appears. Then he looked past me and said, Right, Johnny. Doesn't that fork always appear? Best friends, you gonna end up with that fork. It's gonna happen. You put trust in his basket, and the other guy the same amount of trust in your basket, and one of the baskets is gonna *feel* too fucking heavy. It's simple physics. Now don't get me wrong. I'm not relating this directly to your story. I mean, you and Philpot. What do I know? For all I know he screwed you over *because* you pulled him off the ice. Maybe you should look at it that way. You might've done yourself a favor and left him to sink like a stone. The way I see it, I should've let Kenny die before I had to kill him. On a roof we were running from some punks and had to make a jump to another building. Nothing we hadn't done a million times before, and then he got snagged on an air vent or something, lost his footing, and ended up—fuck if I really know how it happened, I didn't see it—hanging from the ledge, like in a movie. I got his hands and hauled him up and we did what you did. I mean hugged and held each other. Kenny said,

You saved my life. I said, I didn't do anything you wouldn't do. He said: Still, you saved my life. And now when I think about it I knew right then on the roof that I'd probably have to kill him if he kept talking like that. I eventually had to tell him. I said, Kenny, stop saying you owe me your life. I don't want hear it. You don't owe me a thing. Then a few years passed. I mean time went along, and we were doing a sit-and-wait on a guy who owed big on a horse at the raceway. We were in the car for about twelve hours, waiting for this guy to come out, and we got bored. So Kenny starts going back to the old days and ends up talking about that time he almost died and how I helped him out and all, and I knew right then, in the car, that I'd have to kill him. It was in the cards. Just by virtue of the fact that I knew he couldn't go on owing anyone so much without taking something from me. That's the way it works, Sullivan said, and then he stopped speaking and stared at me. The room was getting dark. So what I'm seeing is Philpot fucked you over, but only to give you the excuse you need to kill him. You don't see it that way, but it's that way if you look close enough. Believe me, give it long enough and you're going to feel it in your bones. Now, I'd like you to look at it from my perspective. Don's a good feed. I feed him lines and he legitimizes deals and feeds me a take and we both part ways until the next feed appears. If something doesn't happen to you, it'll happen to him, and I'm not sure I can afford that. Sullivan drilled his eyes at me and said: I could kill you now, right here, but that's not my style. You came to me and I asked you to talk. It's not my style to kill a guy who was asked to tell a story and told it. I've got other ways of doing things, he said, vaguely, and then he made a gesture and the old man put his hand on my shoulder and we walked through the smell of shoe polish (and maybe gun oil. I swear, Morrison, I smelled gun oil), and then I was outside in the wintry twilight. Right then, standing there, I understood that I was either a man who was going to be killed by Sullivan, or a man who, by some good fortune, was going to live into old age, unless I died of some other cause. Weirdly enough, Morrison, I felt better knowing that the two possibilities were in play. On the train home I felt the weight on me lifting. The river outside was flowing with steely resolve. My options, which before the meeting had seemed innumerable and impossible to pin down, suddenly seemed delightfully few and clear.

As I write this, Ann is asleep upstairs. I just checked on my son, and he was asleep, too, making his little snoozy sound, with the faint twilight coming into his room through the window. Everything, right now, is safe and cozy.

EL MORRO

You see, some goddess or something lived in this lake, back when it was freshwater, and then she got tired of the place and fled north and took most of the water with her, and now these natives make yearly barefoot pilgrimages down to this muddy hole and dip leaves into the brine and lick them the way you'd lick a lollipop, or something like that, he said, and he continued talking while the desert slid past, slowly, it seemed, because the horizon was so far off and only things that were close zipped by, and she tried hard to avoid looking at the edge of the road, keeping her eye as far out in the desert as possible, letting him go on with whatever subject was at hand. There were four main strands that formed the litany of his thinking. First and foremost was drugs of all forms and types, their histories and medicinal uses, and their abused uses, on which he was even more of an expert—in particular acid, marijuana, and crystal, his favorite topic and his favorite drug. He talked about drugs as they left his cabin, east of Santa Cruz, all the way down the Pacific Coast Highway, through Los Angeles and out to Palm Springs.

On the way through Joshua Tree, where there was nothing but bare land and a few trees, as far as he could see, he shifted course, and began talking about native culture and native history, his words bent and twisted through his claim (false) that he had native blood, just a generation removed, and that he was related to one of the AIM leaders, a total sellout who could be seen on occasion in bit movie roles, one of those silent Indian types, you know, with the furrowed brow and the hawk eyes, who scrutinize the horizon with the slightly bemused expression you get when you've been betrayed so many times you're no longer betrayed. Eventually, he fixed on the Zuni Pueblo tribe (My true passion. I mean that), and went on for hours, his voice light and airy as he altered history to please his ear, until the Zuni were not only worshippers of deep pits, navels (Yes, fucking navels!), in which their souls and histories were prefabricated, but also stargazers who could see the future with ninety-nine-point-nine-percent accuracy. He talked about a holy seer named Don Juan. Not the fake one, who had supposedly helped Carlos Castaneda along the road to a cosmic experience back in the sixties (Not! Not! Not! he said, slamming the wheel), but, rather, a true visionary named Juan, a Yaqui elder who really knew his shit. (He wasn't a Zuni, but, God damn it, he should have been one!) As he continued talking, his voice trapped in the car, she searched the landscape for trees and tried to tune out his voice, to reduce his words to background noise, like the slipstreamed air coming through the open window.

He talked about birds, his key obsession being hawks, falcons, and falconry, a subject he seemed able to expound on for long stretches, despite his limited knowledge, theorizing about the homing instinct and the pleasure that birds found in their ability to ride the thermals that bloomed from the desert in the afternoon. He stared out at the road and waxed poetic about the way birds flew, the prowess they exuded, saying, Man, those fuckers home in and find a victim from ten miles up, catching the slightest movement, and then dive sightless, eyes closed against the dust and wind, using pure motion and nothing but motion until they're right on top of the kill. You'd be hard-pressed to know which side of the story to look at, because it all meets up right there when the bird hits the prey and the prey, which wasn't anything, man, becomes something, for a second at least, and then suddenly it's nothing but a half-dead carcass being lifted into the sky. Let me put it another way. One second some rodent is poking around obliviously in the weeds, and the next he's being dragged into the sky in a storm of wings, he said. Then he fell into an unusually long silence—while the desert rolled past, the rubble and sage rough in the setting sun—and she figured he was thinking about his brother, Stanley, who had, according to a story he'd told her back at his cabin in Santa Cruz, during their first night together, met his Maker in the early days of the Iraq War in the form of a wayward Air Force missile, a targeting error. My brother died over there, he'd said. He looked up into the sky and saw it coming. At least for a split second, he knew what was going to hit him, man. You always know what's gonna hit you. Maybe for only a sliver of a second. But you still know. Every second, there's a missile ready to strike you in the head.

His fourth topic was more obtuse—at least, she thought so. It was vague, difficult to pin down. When he got started on the fourth topic, as they headed to Tucson (Got a deal to close down there. Business draws me south), she tried to find new, creative ways to avoid listening, putting her fingers in her ears, humming softly to herself, because his fourth topic was her story, and, since he didn't have much to go on in the way of details, he made up most of it from the few facts she had given him back in California: I'm an Illinois girl, she had explained to him on their first night together. My father was a farmer outside Springfield. He tossed me out of the house. They were in bed, smoking a joint, listening to the wind sigh through the second-growth redwoods. Don't say another word, he'd said. Don't say anything else. That's all I need to hear. I'll take the story from there. I really mean it. Not another word. I'd rather fill in the blanks. (Right then she had felt herself adjusting to his way of thinking, drawing on her months on the street, finding a place for him among the characters she'd met: junkies who took in a question and sucked on it for a few minutes before giving a response that seemed far off the mark, as if they were responding to whatever you'd uttered by combining it with some other, more weighty problem; meth freaks who'd answered a question before you even finished asking it and then, overjoyed at their precision and their mystic abilities, fell into blank funks of rage when you shook your head or corrected them; lonely drifter girls who spun monologues of torment and grief that were beautiful in their vivid details, evoking high-tension wires singing in the wind, fathers with hard fists and groping fingers, sexual organs against the thigh, confusion in dimly lit parking garages. For example, one afternoon, in the hills above Hollywood, not far from the horse stables at Griffith Park—an occasional snort or harness jangle could be heard—her friend Kimberly had told her a story that included a blurry-eyed trek through the suburbs of Chicago; an Oak Park businessman named Smith who had taken her under his wing for a few weeks; a gang of bikers in South Dakota who'd plied her with drugs and then put her through a gauntlet of hairy legs. I was somewhere out in Utah, Kimberly had said. I was alone. Someone dropped me off out there. The wind was blowing dust up into the sky. Then this thing appeared—I guess you'd call it a dervish. The thing began talking. It told me a story that went like this:

A guy was out walking in the desert one day when he came upon a horse and a dog. The horse gave a whinny. Then another whinny. Then the dog barked at the horse, and the horse gave yet another whinny. As the man got closer to the animals, he found himself able to understand the particulars of this exchange. All this talk of running free, of eating wild grass, of drinking from freshwater lakes means nothing to me, the dog said. I'm waiting for you to talk about hunting a rabbit, about tearing meat from a bone, about blood and gore. And the horse said, I'm sick of hearing about blood and gore. I'm tired of your stories about sniffing out wild muskrats. I'm waiting to hear you talk of wild clover, of fresh juniper leaves. Then the man felt compelled to interject. Meat and grass. What's the difference? The function of each is to give you life. Without that function, you're just bones. Then both animals turned on the man. The dog tore at his legs, and the horse drove his hooves into his face. When the man was dead, they went back to their argument.

Kimberly told one dervish story after another that afternoon in Griffith Park, reciting them until they both drifted asleep, only to awaken, later, to bright sun and blue sky and the hard clomp of hooves. Above them, on a string of horses led by a guide, was a group of Japanese tourists taking snapshots of a vista that included Hollywood buried in a bowl of haze, the desert landscape, and two homeless girls, pale and gaunt, huddled on a sheet of cardboard.)

•

As they drove north from Tucson through the eggplant pre-dawn light the next morning, after he'd closed the deal (Stay in the room. Don't go anywhere. Don't think. Don't talk to yourself. Don't answer the phone. Don't pray. Don't answer the door), his voice turned dreamy and light while he riffed on her story, saying, You spent a summer sleeping on the sidewalk or in cut-rate hotels with other kids who'd embraced a mute acquiescence in a common dream of freedom, a possible salvation in the form of a good time, hanging on an edge of chance that might at any moment give way to complete, abject reality, and it did, man, it did. It gave way to freeways and faceless drivers behind the glare of windshields backed up anxiously near the Hollywood Bowl, watching as you walked by, one more piece of roadside trash sauntering by in the hot sun, making her way down Highland Avenue, wending her way to the Santa Monica Pier. That was all that was left when I found you. Everything else was gone, pushed away, because you'd come to realize, no, scratch that, you'd learned through trial and error that your only recourse was to forget your past. You had to forget everything. You had to forget the house back in Springfield. You had to forget your father's meaty hands. You had to forget the taste of corn. You had to forget the smell of the barn. You had to forget your mother's wince. You had to forget the fumbling fingers. That was all you had when I found you. Everything else was gone, pushed into the pinhole of the moment. Said moment including the guy who yelled an obscenity at you from his car near the

Hollywood Bowl. Said moment including a guy named Lenny, me, who introduced himself to you with a few pointed but polite questions and then offered you a ride, saying he'd get you out of the city and give you a chance to see a few birds, some redwoods . . .

She found a space wide enough between his words, slipped into it, and fell asleep, only to wake to find him drifting off topic for the first time in days, saying, Look over there, to your left is the biggest copper mine in North America. Those trucks you see crawling up those haulage roads—if you can call them roads—are as big as a house, and down there in the dust those dragline scoopers are ten stories high, with bucket loaders big enough to hold a school bus. There's all kinds of terror involved in running an operation like that. Each guy carries his own unique fear when he creeps up one of those roads. He puts on the earmuffs, leans into the wheel, and prays to God he won't be able to hear, because if someone hits a sensitive vein, or digs too eagerly, the ground gives way and the road crumbles. There's a mine down in South America that comes close in raw output, but it has nothing on *this* one when it comes to history—because this pit started out as a one-man, pick-and-shovel operation. Whereas the mine down south was located through satellite surveillance and mapped by geophysicists who foresaw everything before a single blade cut the earth, I guess you could say this one started out as a pipe dream, a tiny whisper of hope clawing at the ground for more than fifty years until it found itself the way you see it now, which is to say a canyon so deep that hawks and other birds see it and think, That's a good spot to drift over for a while, where I can fly level with the land while still securely high. The South American mine is on holy land guaranteed to give payback in the form of some catastrophic event, most likely in a hundred-year rainfall-slash-flood-slash-mudslide, he said, slowing the car and craning his neck to catch another look at the mine before the road swung to the left, cut along the back side of a town—just a few ramshackle establishments—and then, gaining elevation, entered a deep cut in the stone where they came upon a woman in the middle of the road, dressed in a bright fluorescent vest, wielding an enormous stop sign in one hand and a walkie-talkie in the other.

A fountain of bleached-blond hair cascaded from her watch cap down the shoulders of her canvas coat. She brandished her sign, spoke into the radio, and then came to the car, leaned over, and presented a face: wind-burned and thin, with a scar along one cheek. (That's a knife scar, she'd explain later. I pad foundation on it in the mornings, but it's too deep to cover. I got this one on my honeymoon in Tijuana, when my husband showed me his true nature for the first time. Lucky for me, the blade hit my jawbone and gave me a chance to get away. I've got a baby back there who can't be left for long but might do well just having a few days with her grandmother, she'd say in the car, before instructing Lenny on how to handle the road, telling him, Turn hard here, or Turn easy and ease up, Leadfoot, as they gained elevation and bands of snow stretched from the sheer rock to their left all the way to the edge on the right, cutting clean into a vista that was fantastic and grand, stretching, ochre and sunlit, all the way back to Arizona.) But when the lady leaned into the car for the first time, all she offered was a dull, officious face as she told them they'd have to wait another half hour, at least, for the cleanup crew to finish sweeping off the mountain road ahead, and then she returned to her spot and stood holding the sign.

I like that lady, he said, pouring a cup of coffee from his

thermos, raising it in a toast to the windshield. That lady out
there, that beautiful creature, has endured hour upon hour
alone up here at the entrance to the pass because she probably has Zuni blood of some sort—something Indian, I'd say—
and a stoic ability to put her woes aside and center in on the
moment at hand, to withstand the elements for the sake of
some larger vision. I'd guess she has a little brother with cancer,
a kid named Kenny, or Johnny, or Frankie, and she's working
traffic control in the hope of bumping up to a better job, driving a sweeper, a cozy warm cab with snow falling outside and
a wiper blade clearing a clean swath across the glass. Most
likely, she has another brother, an older one, who works back
at the copper mine. He didn't know he was going to spend his
life doing that kind of work. But one day he got a call from the
mine office and a guy said, We're ready to hire you, come on
down. We've processed your papers. And he said, What
papers? And the guy said, The ones you put in. And the brother,
Bobby or Ronny or Sammy, said he'd accept the job, but he
was confused because he hadn't put in an application. Then
his father and his oldest brother, named something like Mike
and Mike Jr., came home from work, washed the dust off their
faces, and said, You get any news? He said, Yeah, I got some
fucking news. I just got a call from the mine office and I'm being hired, but I didn't put in papers for a job. I was planning
to go down to Tucson for work. And the father and the older
brother said, We put the papers in for you. That's the way it
works in this family. And this guy—let's settle on the name
Bobby—couldn't say no. Bobby felt himself caught in the long
history of his family. Past generations had opened up an obligation. So he said, What the hell, and this was five years ago—
and he is still there today, knowing that he'll spend the rest of
his life driving a dump, or, if he's bumped up, operating a

shovel, not so much because he's resigned himself to fate, though that's part of it, but mainly because when he's finished each day, his arms aching and his brain rattled from the fear he gets every time he drives one of those ramp roads, he's too tired to think about reinventing his life. Lenny toasted the windshield again with his coffee while the woman with the stop sign gazed at them, then she carefully laid down her sign, walked over to his window, and said, Mind if I have a sip of that coffee? He offered her the cup, waited for her to take a sip, then held his palm and the pill out the window, and said, How about a little pick-me-up to go with the sip? And she said, Don't mind if I do, and closed her fingers gently over the pill.

·

By the time they came down out of the mountain pass, crossed the New Mexico line, and hit the lower elevations, things had switched around. She was in the back seat, doing her best to avoid hearing Lenny, while the lady with the stop sign was in the front seat listening attentively as he talked with delusional precision, saying, I guarantee you're going to meet my hawk, Jag, because he's the best motherfucking bird in the world, and the lady laughed and said, I'd love to meet Jag, and he said, That bird's got intense focus. I mean, he can fly out of my sight, but he always keeps me in his sight, and when he's ready he'll dive out of the sky and land on my arm as gently as a feather, and the lady laughed again while outside the car the pines gave way to scrub and brush and the road straightened itself out and sliced the desert into two equally desolate parts. He's actually above us right now. He's following along but keeping a discreet distance, he said, and then the lady, trying to get a word in edgewise, said, My husband swore he'd come back to get me. He said he'd come at me with a gun. And he did. He came back one night and stood out on the lawn shouting. He told me to get out there. He told me to be a man, and I told him I'm a woman, and he said that didn't matter, he was going to treat me like a man. Then he shot out the picture window, and the police came and hauled him away. Now he's down in the state prison in Winslow. He and a million just like him.

By the time they came out of the mountains and entered the Zuni reservation, Lenny and the lady in the front seat were like two souls united by a mutual need formed back during the two hours they'd spent navigating the treacherous hairpin turns and windblown snow, arguing about how to manage the wheel in a skid. The lady had said, The myth is that you turn into the skid, but up here in these mountains you've got no choice but to turn against the skid as hard as you can and hope the wheels help the brakes. Believe me, I know what I'm talking about. I've driven this pass a hundred times and I've seen what happens to trucks that turn into a skid. They head over the edge. Even the big trucks, and I'm talking about the ones my brother drives, turn into a wad of tinfoil when they hit the bottom . . .

By the time they were down the straightaway and in the heart of the reservation, he and the lady seemed like lovers of a sort, easy in their manner, stopping the car for a roadside picnic (You stay in the car. Get some rest. Leave us be. We need some time alone, he whispered), sharing a sandwich, passing it back and forth, sipping coffee, talking softly while she watched them from the car. Finally, the best she could do was close her eyes and listen to the sound of their voices, coming through the air as if across a great distance. The best she could do was block their voices by remembering the way the road had felt, suddenly smooth and serene, straightening it-self like a magic carpet beneath the wheels after the hours of twisty mountains. When the sound of their voices stopped, she opened her eyes and looked out to see them kissing, while behind them the vast expanse of desert threw itself almost as far as the eye could see, but not quite, because on the hori-zon, just about lost in the haze, a plateau hunched submis-sively beneath a huge, vacant sky.

As they passed through a reservation town, the lady in the front seat grew silent, and he took over the conversation once again, saying, They walk a hundred miles to pay their respects to Old Lady Salt, who ran away from Black Rock Lake. She took most of the potable water with her and left behind a use-less briny soup. Now they go there once a year and plant their prayer sticks in what's left of the lake and draw up granules of salt and bag them and take them back home to rim the glasses of margaritas—or whatever the fuck they do with it, man, because it isn't just salt but something else, even better than salt, he said, and then the lady broke in, saying, My brother loves margaritas. He's gorgeous, he's incredible-looking. He's out in Hollywood. He's going to be a star. Let me tell you. He really is. He has the gumption. He's a dreamer. He has stars in his eyes. My big brother gave him shit about it, told him he was nuts, and then he signed him up for a job at the mine. So my little brother went and worked there for a few weeks, until one of the terraces gave out. He was driving a dump and the road just folded away in front of him. He came home that night and told my father he wasn't fit for that kind of work. He said he had a vision and was going to follow it no matter what, and then he packed up and left. He sends me cards, and I have this picture of him, she said, taking a photo out of her pocket, unfolding it carefully, holding it up into his line of vision so that he could see and drive at the same time. A long, lean face with cool dark eyes and hair slicked back tight against his skull. The boy in the photo was frowning slightly, with his jaw locked as if he had bitten something sour. There was remorse, or something that looked like remorse, in his eyes. But there was hope, too. Lenny snatched the photograph from her and said, Yeah, he's good-looking. He has a bit of Gregory Peck and a hint of Clark Gable and, what the hell, a bit of James Dean, but let me tell you what's going to happen to him. Let me give you the truth. He's going to fall onto the streets along with the rest of them and end up holding a spoon over a flame. He's going to slip into the cracks and you won't hear of him again until word arrives that his body was found in some empty lot up in the hills, if you're lucky, or in front of La Brea Tar Pits if you're not, because no one wants to die in front of a tourist from Wisconsin. No one wants to shatter the congenial blandness they bring, that greenhorn belief in hopes and dreams that settles like the smog and makes it exhilaratingly hard to breathe. And let me tell you, there is nothing better in this world than struggling to breathe. Nothing. Nothing. Nothing, he said, and then the lady began an argument, and the first lively round of bickering began, a tight but somehow still loving exchange that, with the window wide open and her head against the back seat, faded off into nothing more than a pattern of clicks, wooden in nature, continuing until the engine died, and they left her asleep in the car.

•

She woke to find the neat formality of a clean park, all paved paths and carefully placed signs indicating the names of the

trees and the bushes around the huge stone mesa, with a waterfall, gone dry for the winter, just a tongue of mineral deposits
starting wide near the top, where a few trees clung, and thinning
as it neared the bottom. She got out of the car and started
walking. To her left was some kind of visitors' center, with
floor-to-ceiling windows. She could hear his voice floating
along a trail and she paused for a moment to look far up the
rock face to where trees had sprouted from windblown seeds
that had landed in the wrong place at the wrong time, a crack,
a crag in the stone, and then, left with no other choice, had
grown, bending, angling for the sunlight, finding odd posi-
tions, and holding on for dear life. Men came here astonished
at the immensity of the stone formation, he was saying when
she got within earshot. She stopped on the path and listened.
They stumbled here in wonderment. How could something
like this rise out of so much flatness? It's the work of the
Devil, some said. The work of God, others said. Obviously
they all—and I mean every damned gimp-legged wanderer—
felt compelled to make a mark on this thing, he said, pointing
to the petroglyphs. To scratch their names, to leave some
indication that they had existed.

They chiseled, as you can see, carefully—the early ones—
and then went off to die of thirst, or to reconsider their failings,
or to enslave Mexico, or to be enslaved. Depending on the
luck of the draw. Now there are laws against leaving your
mark, he said. You can't even spit on the face of this rock or
some guard will emerge from the visitors' center back there
with a club in his hand. I know, because I tried it last time
I was here. I marked my name with a pen and ended up incar-
cerated. He arched his head and held his hand to his brow in
a salute against the sun and then turned back to examine the

stone, reaching out across the fence as if to touch it, wiggling his fingers in the air. The wind was rising. The sun buried itself in the rubble. He cleared his throat and took a few steps backward, then opened his arms as if to embrace the scene before preparing to speak again. He braced his shoulders and set his feet while the stop-sign lady, to his left, did the same.

No one else was around. The cold had emptied the tourists out. In a firm, hard voice, he spoke directly to the monument of his country's urgent need for redemption; he spoke of birds who fly in the depths of night skies, trying to find some distant pull of gravity in the darkness, flying wing to wing in V formations; he spoke of forlorn tribes licking salt from their wounds, tender-footing secretly from one sacred site to the next, searching for some lost part of their history; he spoke of cookhouses in Washington State, tucked deep in the wilds, cranking out pure sacramental salts. Then, while she stood a few yards down the path, listening to his words bounce off the rock, flat and solid, forced into what seemed to be a tight, unavoidable vortex, he turned, pointed, and began to tell her story again, saying, You never dreamed you'd end up in a place like this. You never saw it ending this way. It just didn't occur to you. How could you dream this up? On the streets of L.A. there just isn't room for this kind of monument to the past. When you were wandering Sunset, locked in that haze, your capacity to imagine this kind of place just didn't exist. It took a man like me to get you out of there and to carry you here, he said. And now it's going to take a man like me to make you really see it in all of its splendor. I'm not trying to grandstand. I'm just stating the facts as I see them. Back on those streets, you dreamed of dogs and cats, of a nice little house. But never anything like this, he said, and his voice grew soft and he whispered something to the stop-sign lady. Then he turned back and said, This is a fitting place to end this thing we've had.

•

Behind the desk in the visitors' center the ranger—his name was Russell—watched the visitors on the video monitors, scrutinizing the way they moved. A woman with a shock of blond hair hunched her shoulders and rocked on her heels. Next to her, a tall man with stovepipe legs threw fists of gravel into the weeds and stepped with the eager jitteriness he'd seen in punks who came out to vandalize the park, white boys who had lost, or never had, respect for their place in the world. (No, not their place in the world but the reality of the world to begin with.) He liked the view he got on the screens—black-and-white, low quality—how it made folks look all the more ghostly and unsuspecting. An element of desecration was caught by these four cameras: one mounted with a view from the visitors' center, another on a post in the parking lot. (Campers. People trading drugs, rubbing against each other as they made the exchange. Families stiff from the road, stretching their limbs, rotating their heads and bending over to touch toes. Once or twice a year, a few nuns in habits. Once, two monks, from Vietnam, draped in orange robes. Fellow Zuni, always recognizable somehow—something in the bend of their legs, the lope of their gait, a slight hunch in the back of the older ones, a confusion of reverence and weariness.) Another camera was on a tree up the path and showed people pausing to examine the monument before it closed in on them. The last camera was on the rock itself—a small unit, wedged in a crag, with a fish-eye lens that spread the image. Years of observing the screens (when he wasn't out on foot patrol) had given him a pretty good ability to draw speculative conclusions, as he watched people wander across the parking lot, disappear out of view, and then show up, a moment later, on the path. He could spot a vandal in the particular way he put out a cigarette, dropping it to the sidewalk and grinding it. (Vandals smoked. All of them.)

He had watched these two saunter up the path. The punk had spread his arms, opening them wide and holding them out before letting them flop back down to his sides. That gesture had clued him in to the nature of the situation, he later reflected. There was a carelessness in the way the punk had let his arms drop down after opening them to embrace the scene. Whites did that. They seemed incapable of allowing a sustained calm into the way they moved. Meanwhile, on the parking-lot screen, a third figure, a girl, got out of the car alone and looked warily around, trying to get her bearings. Right off, he knew her type: pale, spiritless, with bony hips. A third wheel with unkempt, wind-tangled hair. There was a deliberation—or was it simply exhaustion?—in the way she reached out to touch the plaques as she walked down the path, fingered the branches of the trees, and stopped for a minute to stare up at the stone.

Later, Russell would look back and rehash and reexamine the way things had transpired, testing his intuitive abilities, remembering how the three of them had stood there—the guy talking, wagging his hands in the air, going on and on, while the woman, the one with blond hair, leaned forward and listened attentively. The girl—the third wheel—stood back, waiting to approach while the guy continued to talk for five minutes, maybe more, moving up to the fence and pointing to one of the markings. (A vandal testing his impulses. The urge to deface seemed evident in his gestures.) Finally the guy turned and addressed the third-wheel girl, talking to her while she shook her head slightly, reaching up to dab a tear or to wipe something from her eye, and then he and the woman simply walked away together, back down the path to the parking lot, where he could see them getting into the car, starting it up, and tearing away, leaving behind a cloud of dust and smoke.

When he got to the girl, she was leaning over the fence, resting her belly on the wood rail, using the leverage of her body to drive a piece of flagstone into the rock, carving out a single line as hard as she could, grunting slightly as her feet lifted up with each clean stroke. One more soul trying to leave a mark in the stone. At least fifteen a year came through with spray cans and indelible markers and attempted, as best they could, to match the elegant demarcations of the past. He'd seen it all. But, stepping around the corner and finding her there, he saw in the delicacy of her action and in the lift of her toes a balletic movement, and he knew something about her that he wasn't sure how to articulate, so he made his command a bit softer than usual and held his billy club down at his side as he approached. When she turned, he saw the face of a girl who had lost almost everything, including her ability to speak. She kept the mute silence of a soothsayer. He saw that right away. It wasn't the willed silence of the guilty. Her lips were loose against her teeth, not pressed tight. Her eyes weren't holding back words. Her eyebrows refused movement. Most in the white world didn't understand medicine people, he thought, seeing her. (This wasn't one of the usual irrelevant thoughts that came to his mind when he saw tourists wandering around, gawking, showing disrespect not only for the place they were in but for themselves, too, in the way they walked, wobble-footed, talking too loud and looking too quickly.) In truth, a medicine man never picked his vocation. It was a fate that was bestowed, forcing one to forsake certain pleasures in the world—he thought—in order to become someone who knew a little too much about reality.

•

She was about as white as you could get, he told his wife. I mean as white as a ghost, junkie-white, with hardly any blood, and that made it hard for me to blame her, to pin the crime on her, so to speak. And, anyway, her sidekicks took off on her. She didn't look drunk or high and just seemed to need help. He was telling the story in bed, late at night. He knew he was getting to his wife's heart by telling a good-deed story. She liked it when he told stories that put him in a kind light. He had driven the girl up to Grants and hooked her up with the social worker there and she had promised to get her whatever help was available and a bed in the wayward house for vagrant types—or whatever the hell they call that place, he explained, sighing softly. He lay back and let his wife kiss him and conjured up a clear view of what he saw each day at work, because it had been such a persistent part of his world, for so long, that he saw it—really saw it—only when he was at home, in bed, drowsy with sleep. Then it arose, full-blown, in a vision of grandeur and hope, with the waterfall—in spring—spilling madly down the face of the rock, filling the pool, holding itself against the dryness and the dust.

Just before drifting off, he had one last thought. Maybe he'd keep the mark she had made on the stone a secret and leave it there until the archaeologists from Santa Fe, who came in once or twice a year, took notice. Then he'd try to persuade them that it had been there for years and wasn't worth the trouble of fixing, because the patch material—the limestone-colored compound they used in these cases—would be more noticeable, an eyesore, one more modern distraction for those who came to look. It's just a scratch, he'd say. A few years of wind and rain will blow it away with all the others. It would go against his good judgment and the strictures of his job and the park itself to lie for her sake, he thought. And with that he fell asleep, carrying with him the monument, his tribal land, and the rest of the world.

THE BUTLER'S LAMENT

He could be seen wandering the paths in front of the main building, walking stiffly with his arm out and his hand extended, holding an imaginary platter on his palm, moving around the hospital grounds with dainty steps and mumbling to himself. (I'd not judge you, dear sir, not one whit, for ravishing the ladies of the village, sir.) He had a stiff formality in those moments, standing alone, one more soul cut loose from his former life, trying to establish a presence under the arching trees; one more patient amid many, shuffling around with a kind of benign gentility that was disorienting to the staff members, myself included. For the most part, we ignored his long soliloquies about the inelegant desperation of the flesh compared with the elegance of precise work. As with many of the patients, the nurses had given him a nickname—the Butler. As a professional, I resisted using nicknames, but eventually even I began calling him the Butler, because he so firmly inhabited the delusion, claiming that he had been a butler to Lord Leitrim, or Lord Byron—he vacillated between the two when he was in his primary delusional state, and suffered fits that shattered the decorum of his usual, rather quiet self, sending him into convulsively amplified butler gestures. He would place his open hand on his midriff and bow violently forward until his head came close to touching the ground. (At your service, sir! I'd get you the tea, sir, if you'd be so kind as to loosen the restrictions of these garments.) All the while, presumably, he still remembered his former days as a tool-and-die man out of Detroit.

One morning, behind the main building, near the loading dock, he spoke to me in his normal voice, in which a hint of Irish lilt was blended with workaday Detroit. You're the boss, Doc, he said, and I said, Yes, I guess you could put it that way. I'm the head of the hospital. You bring us in when we wander around the paths, he said, and I said, I suppose when I feel so inclined I do order a nurse to go and get you. You're the looming boss, he said, and I waited a few beats—it was midsummer, and the breeze brushed the willow branches with a broom-sweeping sound—before I said, I suppose you're right, although I try not to loom. And he said, Well, you can't help but loom if you're a boss. And then for a moment I thought he was going to fall into his delusional states. (He was leaning his head against the chain-link fence, holding on to it with his arms out, gazing into the ravine.) He said, I've had my share of looming. And I said, Well, I'd like to hear about it if you feel like talking. He said, I came over to this country when I was ten. I was raised with a heavy hand. My father was my first looming boss. He loomed like hell, he said. I've had others, he said, gripping the fence.

Yes, I've had my share of looming bosses, Doc. We had a machine at the factory that would grip the door and align it, hold it in position while a nozzle swung into a predrilled hole and injected foam. The foam made the door soundproof and strengthened it. These were heavy-duty doors for use in schools and sports stadiums. Anyway, one day a door was in the foam machine and the nozzle was missing the hole and spraying all over the place. I went down the production line to the foam-injection station and began to tinker with the mechanism. As a tool-and-die man, you're bound to precise measurements, but when you're on the line and trying to keep things moving, you end up tinkering. That's the strange part of the job, the fact that being a tool-and-die guy means you're trained to make fine machines. When you're an apprentice, they say, Look, kid, from now on your life is going to be about precision. But then you go from grinding precision dies to moving up the ladder, and up the ladder means adjusting equipment in an assembly plant, and that means, as I said, tinkering. (But you're still called a tool-and-die guy, you see. You still have the burden of title.) In any case, when I got there the nozzle was spastically groping around for a hole. Tapping itself against the top of the door and spraying wildly. There are four laser beams that scan the door and feed data into the computer, and then the padded arms come out to embrace it, gently, while another beam locates the holes along the top and another, smaller computer guides the nozzle into each one. But like I said, the nozzle groped and sprayed the foam all over the place, which by the time I got there was beginning to co-agulate. Anyway, as I leaned down and tried to get to the control box, which was buried in foam, I felt the boss behind me. (You get used to feeling your boss behind you on the line.) Feeling the boss behind me wasn't a big deal, normally, but in this case I felt him—not sure how to put this, Doc, not sure I even have words for it—looming in a new way—not sure if *new* is right—in a heavy way—maybe that's the right word, *heavy*—and I turned to find him there. His name was Jenson and he was a big man with cold eyes and a tight, scrunched-up face. He was a heavy drinker, Jenson. He had a bottle of schnapps on the job with him most of the time. He'd been getting away with it, but he was approaching the end. That's how it works: You become a boss, you turn to the bottle to deal with the pressure, and then you use your position (as boss) to hide the drinking until you're subservient to it (the drinking), and then eventually the new boss (liquor) fires you and you're spit out onto the streets of the city, where you drift around waiting for someone or something else to loom over your shoulder, because to be honest, Doc, a man needs to feel that now and then to stay steady on his feet. Anyway, that day on the line I felt the looming, but it was different. I turned and looked at him, and he said, You idiot, you threw the adjustment off on this machine, and I said, No, sir, I had nothing to do with it, and I turned back to tinkering with the box, looking down into it, holding my screwdriver, poking, doing the best I could to look efficient and precise, carefully avoiding the fuses. I had an awareness deep inside that the door's misalignment had nothing to do with mechanics, but instead with the data feed and the thinkers (as I like to sometimes call the computers). I now know that even as a precision tool-and-die guy I couldn't have adjusted the machine properly because the actual physical machine wasn't the problem. It was the thinking part that was off. I now see that Jenson probably understood this fact himself, which might account not only for the way he loomed over me but also for the way I, in turn, felt a desire to loom back, so to speak, although I was still leaning over the box, poking with a screwdriver and saying, loudly,

over the noise of the machine, Let's see, maybe if I just carefully bring this to a gradation of two point five, or, Let me ad-
just this a fraction of a point. Of course, part of any job is to
look like you're doing the job, and to pretend to be exact even
when in truth you're never going to get close to the ideal point
of precision. You learn pretty early in your apprenticeship that
micrometers are meant for show. A master tool-and-die man
becomes proficient in a kind of precision showmanship that
covers up the deficiencies of being human, and that's exactly
the kind of show I was putting on when the nozzle swung out
in its ghostly way—with that weird robotic semblance of humanity, looking decisive and clearheaded at one moment and
then hesitant and contemplative the next—aligned itself with
Jenson's face, and hovered there for a second or two, as if it
were taking aim, while Jenson stared back at it with his accusatory boss stare. Then the nozzle sprayed him full in the
face: a great gush of foam that sent him stumbling back, splut-
tering and moaning the way he did when he was drunk near
the end of his shift. Needless to say, he fired me on the spot.
He said, You're fired. Get your back pay and clean out your
locker. You're finished! Kaput! I've had enough of you. He was
sure that I no longer cared as much about the machines as I
did about my own sense of looming in relation to him. He
knew damn well that although I was putting on a pretense of
tinkering, of making an adjustment, I'd had nothing to do with
the fact that the nozzle had swayed toward his face and taken
aim in a human manner. I'm now sure that he understood that
the machine itself had had everything to do with it, and that
I had nothing to do with it, and that the two worlds, the machine and the human, had somehow traded places, so that
what the machine had done to Jenson was exactly what I

would've done if I had been a foam nozzle. He understood this and responded in kind, making sure that he, as a boss, kept the world in an orderly state by firing me for gross imprecision. He wanted to be sure that I was still human—a dejected, fired worker, no longer a tool-and-die man—and the machine was still a machine, blameless. He said it again for good measure, his voice coming tight and angry out of his foam-covered face, Clean out your locker and put in your last time card and get the fuck out of my sight. I don't want to see your face again, he said, and then he began to dig in and expound on my inability to be precise, and how I'd never work in this town again, because my gross imprecision and inability to make careful adjustments, my failings as a tool-and-die man, would soon become widely known. He was still shouting at me as I walked down the line to gather my things. His voice faded into the sound of the machinery—echoing up into the girders high overhead, the cavernous room combining all of the noise into a single deep roar. All that precision! All that inexactitude conjoining in a nonsensical storm of inefficiency to somehow, I dare say, miraculously, produce final products. As I left the plant that afternoon—out into the bright sun—the line had once again ground to a halt, but it would, I knew, soon kick back into production, popping out the doors one after another, each one solid and foam-filled, testifying to the glory of our pretense of control.

·

A few days later, I found the patient back on the path. He stopped and bowed, keeping his head down for a few seconds before snapping up and addressing his master, Lord Byron, or perhaps Lord Leitrim, who would be (I imagined) demanding in a gentlemanly way, expecting attendance to certain corporal needs, a beck-and-call availability, a trust born out of innumerable shared moments: mornings in sleep-warm bedrooms, afternoons in smoky parlors, evenings in serving pantries. After a few minutes, he turned on his heel and walked quickly up the path to the porch, and said, I've come back to inquire about the state of Lord Byron's health. I'm afraid he has consumption. He's coughing up blood, he added, shaking his head gently. Far off, beyond the hospital grounds, cars passed on the road. We were dead in the center of a hot Midwestern afternoon. The air relentlessly still. I took the Butler by the shoulders, pulled him close, put my mouth close to his ear, and said, Lord Byron is fine. He's in good health. You have nothing to worry about. Nothing at all. You'll continue to serve him a long time. Then I watched as he fell into a grand mal seizure of epic proportions, throwing himself forward with gusto, pounding his head against the porch railing until, at my command, the orderlies ran out to restrain him. His tool-and-die days are fucking over. No more of his Detroit shit, one of the men said. And I said, You may be right. Now get him in a restraint and put him in his room.

•

I don't exactly know why, but I felt, and still feel, that his door-factory story was somehow an indictment of my treatment methods, I told Anna during one of our collegial bull sessions a few years later. She sat back for a moment, touched her chin, looked out the window, and said, Well, I think you felt betrayed—if that's the word—by the fact that the two variations of his primary delusional states—serving Lord Byron one day and Lord Leitrim the next—somehow mirrored your own position here at the hospital. You were tired and short on time and decided to simply play into his primary delusion. Lord Byron is dead, you might've said. You were struggling with the theme of servitude that his delusion raised in connection with your own duties as his doctor and, in turn, with the story he'd told you about the factory. She went on in this vein for a while. I hardly listened. She had a lovely soft contralto voice. Her teeth were clean and straight. Her blond hair shimmered. Outside, the other wing of the hospital loomed beneath a cold, wintry sky. I could just make out the top edge of the water tower. Its copper roof was smearing the brick with tongues of blue. Anna touched her hair and paused for a moment and asked me if I agreed, and I said I did. She then gently regurgitated the facts of the case, feeding them to me while I watched her soft, wide mouth. As a boy in Ireland, the patient had visited the estate of Lord Leitrim, not far from his home in Carrick. His mother had had a love of Lord Byron. That explained the dual nature of his otherwise monothematic delusion. Something dreamy had entered Anna's voice. We were accomplices in a grand conspiracy. The enigma of the case flickered between us like a warm fire as she went on and on about the Butler, who had once walked the grounds of the hospital, moving elegantly down the path toward the road, beneath the big diseased elms, and then swung to the right or to the left, depending on his will or perhaps on chance, and had come back toward me as I watched him from the porch, thinking about the story he had told me back behind the building, or just wondering about his proper demeanor in relation to his ruddy, bewhiskered face, the gray stubble and the eyes deep in their sockets. He'd threatened, even then, to fade into the vast array of past cases, each of them—the so-called Executive, the Stock Broker, the

Janitor—seemingly desperate, demanding my energies and time and expertise for a relatively short period and then gradually fading, displaced by another case, so that the man who had been called the Butler and who had for one summer absorbed so much of my attention had since drifted off and away, first into a kind of besieged state of servitude to an imaginary employer who asked him to fetch things from the kitchen and who depended on him in the morning for help with his garments and so on, and then—after the grand mal seizure—simply mimicked the gestural remnants of the profession, the nodding and bowing, and then later simply the bowing, until finally even that was gone and he was just another soul restrained and medicated into a placid compliance with state regulations, left to sit alone on the porch and rock away his few remaining days in relative silence, thumping the warped floorboards with the rails of the chair or simply sitting still while the breeze lifted, or fell, and the clipboards at the nurses' station, jammed with notes and schedules and charts, rattled softly on their hooks.

THE ICE COMMITTEE

It was late afternoon. It would soon be dusk.

"I don't think I ever told you the one with Captain Hopewell in it," the man named Kurt was saying.

"Don't start. For God's sake, you'll jinx us for sure," the man named Merle said. "Just get me thinking about that one and it'll jinx us."

"This one isn't going to jinx us. If you knew the story, you'd know that," Kurt said, and then for a few minutes both men sat silently and mulled over everything they'd discussed on the nature of luck over the course of the last few months as they'd wandered up and down Superior Street, shaking a cup for spare change, scraping for odd jobs, whatever it took to gather enough for some booze and a scratch lottery ticket. They'd agreed that to talk too much about good fortune just before you scratched would decrease the odds of it coming, because luck had to bend around the place and time of the scratch, establishing itself in relation to your state of mind at that particular moment. You either scratched in a deliberately calm, quiet moment, or in one of great emotional intensity.

Scratch a ticket on the sidewalk in front of the Hope Mission—
or worse yet, inside the lounge, with all that dusty grief—no
chance in hell. At your mother's grave on a pristine winter day,
after paying your prayerful respects and laying some flowers
against the tombstone, about fifty-fifty. Out in Lake Superior
on the deck of a good ship under a gloriously crystalline sky,
sixty-forty. On the deck of the same ship in a hundred-year
storm with slush ice forming on the lake, just after hearing the
news that your old man's died, ninety-ten. Back at your mother's
grave in the fall, at dusk, having survived the hundred-year
storm, sure thing. Best to clear the head of all expectation and
settle into a state of not-caring as you look out with silent and
blissful longing at the lake.

"You haven't heard this one, so it's not going to hurt our
chances if I tell it," Kurt was saying, leaning back on the bench.
"It won't change the odds any more than if I were to start talking about that dream I have of buying a decommissioned ship,
either here or down in Cleveland. Dry-dock the fucker, put in
a Jacuzzi and a pool table and a wet bar—all that stuff," he said,
and then the older man, who sat formally with his hands
on his knees, reached up and adjusted the lapels of his coat.

"You just planted a seed in my mind about you buying
that retired ship, which is just as much of a jinx, me thinking it."

"So you're saying I shouldn't talk?" Kurt said.

The lake in front of them was unusually calm for this time
of year, a burnished gleam that stretched out to a single vessel, far out, heading to the horizon. Behind them, to the right,
the bridge sat with its hundred-ton counterweights up—the
span down—waiting stubbornly to be relieved of its burden.
The port of Duluth was dead, the chutes and conveyers empty.

With the exception of the ship out on the water, nothing seemed to move.

"As we've discussed ad infinitum, you should hold off talking too much about fortune—good or bad—until we scratch the ticket," Merle said, shaking his hands in his sleeves and twisting his cuff links into position. He had a long, gaunt face and sad, still periwinkle eyes.

"Well, Captain Hopewell was a hopeless asshole," Kurt said. "Can I at least say that?"

Ships and 'Nam, 'Nam and ships—that's all the kid's got, Merle thought.

"Whatever you say, Professor," Kurt said.

"I didn't say a word," Merle said.

"But you were thinking something and I know what it was," Kurt said. He stood and walked down to the shore to examine, for the second time that afternoon, the dead flies and grime that marked where the water—no tide, nothing resembling a tide—had receded during the hot, dry summer.

The ship had disappeared over the horizon, heading on what seemed to be an upbound tack that would pass to the south of Split Rock Lighthouse and Isle Royale, then charting a course to the Soo Locks (*likely the Poe Lock*, Kurt thought, *yeah, the Poe—it's the only one that could handle a boat that long*), down through Lake Huron, down the St. Clair, past Detroit, across Erie, up the Well and Canal, across Lake Ontario, through the St. Lawrence Seaway—four hundred slogging miles—and out to sea. It was easy to imagine the urgency that would fill a ship this time of year as it shoved through the locks, searching out the sudden serenity of the seaway with the land close on both sides, and then, leaving it behind, entering the Gulf of St. Lawrence and, finally, the open Atlantic. That's how it worked. You boarded in the spring, hung from the sides and painted the hull, scrubbed the deck, and worked your ass off bolting and unbolting hatches, hardly paying the water much notice, until one day, as you stood on the deck having a smoke, the vastness of the open sea hashed you like a girl with her skirt blown up, exposing a beautiful secret, and then you fell back to the boredom—the hatches, the decks, the dust in the holds. It opened and shut on you, the sea did.

"Hopewell, you busted my ass!" Kurt shouted. "You were a vintage Nova Scotia stoic."

"Again, I have to say, I've heard everything I want to hear about Hopewell," Merle said, studying his friend. Kurt was rail thin, dressed in an old flannel shirt and a canvas jacket that hung loosely from his wide shoulders. All the drugs he'd taken had given him a saintly gauntness, as if he'd starved himself for some grand purpose, and his eyes—when he wasn't squinting—had a shifty dart that somehow made him look younger than his fifty-three years.

"Come on, just tell me a little bit, just a word or two to confirm you know the story," Kurt said, slapping his sides and hopping, lifting off his toes. "I think we agreed that it's okay if it's a new version that has good luck in it."

"Well, if you insist," Merle said. "You told me you were working an old scrap heap. 'Due for the heap,' you said. It was flying a Portuguese flag and had a captain named Hopewell. Then you asked me for another word for *hard-ass*, and I suggested you use the word *stoic*. You said, 'Yeah, *stoic*, that's the right word.' You called Hopewell 'a vintage Nova Scotia stoic,' like you just did a minute ago, and then you told me the story."

"I could've told you a hundred fucking Hopewell stories.

I have a bunch of them," Kurt said. "And *stoic*'s a word I knew before you taught it to me."

"'Nam was in it," Merle said.

"I'd say half my stories have 'Nam in them. That doesn't prove to me you've heard this one."

"Well, it had a Captain Hopewell in it, and it had 'Nam in it, and it had a ship that was due for scrap."

"Did it have a guy named Billy-T—my buddy who enlisted with me in Benton Harbor?"

"Did we not agree that we'd restrain from telling stories that might in some way involve luck? Did we not agree, at some point?" Merle said, pounding his walking stick into the dirt.

"Look, just humor me and confirm that you've heard it, and I'll shut up—but if you haven't heard it, then I think I should talk because I feel like talking, and you know if I don't talk when I want to talk there's a possibility that the tension from not talking might jinx us just as much as me telling some kind of story that has the wrong type of luck in it. Was there a guy named Billy-T? If Billy-T was in there, you heard the story before, in which case I'll let it go."

Merle reached up, pinched the dimple in his tie, curled his palm over the end of his stick, and—shaking violently— tried to stand. "Jesus, kid. Don't blame me if this scratch is worthless. I have my own desires to talk, but I also have the wisdom to hold my tongue."

He gave up the effort, sitting again, and watched as Kurt took a chug of beer, wiped his mouth, lit a cigarette, and scuffed his feet as he prepared to tell the story, working it over in his mind (presumably), trying to remember if he had indeed told Merle the entire thing from beginning to end, or if he'd given just an abbreviated version with the end left out.

"I was working as a low-life maintenance monkey on an

old heap, a coal burner out of Cleveland flying a Portuguese flag. I guess I told you that, and maybe I told you that we were heading on a northerly course into some nasty weather. You could feel in the roll of the ship that someone was in for a dose of bad luck," he said, and then he waited for Merle to cut in on him, to warn him again about jinxing the ticket, but the old man had his head back and his eyes closed, nodding softly, so Kurt went on, saying, "I've told you about how it felt, the sense that the water wanted to drag someone to the bottom, and maybe I've told you how I hit Hopewell on occasion with my 'Nam shit as a way to get out of deck duty, and how most of the time he'd just listen and then tell me to get back to work. But this time was different. For one thing, against protocol, the bastard came in and ate with us at our table. The captain and his guys usually eat in a different galley, but I guess he'd noticed a disgruntled tension in the crew. Not that we'd ever mutiny. I mean, it was a good-paying gig. Mutinies are out of style. Anyway, the way I used to deliver it was to put in as much lingo as I could, but keep it vague, too, if you know what I'm saying, and try to ride a balance, because a 'Nam story has to sound crazy and true at the same time. And that day, with that storm churning under the hull, I knew I had to touch some part of Captain Hopewell that he didn't think I could get to, so I softened him up with some random details—the weird, pink flechette powder that dusted our fingers; psyops choppers pumping the sounds of crying babies down on the gooks to drive them to a crazy surrender. I worked these details until Hopewell's face went tight and his mouth screwed and the stick up his ass seemed to nudge against his brow. Then I knew he was truly hearing me.

"I told him that when I turned eighteen I was sure I'd be

drafted and wanted an advantage on which service I'd join, so I enlisted on the buddy program with my best friend, Billy-T— we went over to the recruiting office in Benton Harbor and joined together. Anyway, I could see that Hopewell's eyes were drifting to the porthole, and I felt I had to get to the point, so I jumped right into it and told him how me and Billy-T found ourselves in the hot and heavy in Hue, street-to-street, real-war shit, and how Billy-T—who had a serious lisp—called in air-strike coordinates on the radio net. Mortar rounds coming in all around us, and these shit-can field phones we were using . . . 'Hell, don't get me started on that,' I said to Hopewell. 'Don't get me started on the arms we had over there. For a while we were using—and most folks don't believe me when I tell them this—fucking Remington rifles. I swear, wood stocks, single bore, flint action. You'd break one of those down and you could hardly get it back together because the so-called follower spring in the clip would fuck you up.' I added as much of that bullshit as I could to keep Hopewell's eyes from the porthole, and then I swung back to the main story again, making sure he understood that we weren't used to streets. We were used to a guy taking point with no line of sight. Hue was all line of sight, if you dared to look. You know the deal—put a helmet on your bayonet and stick it up over the wall, watch it get nailed with fire, just a hunk of Swiss cheese when you bring it back down. (Then some Wisconsin newbie would go ahead and do the same.) I told Hopewell, 'See, man, Billy-T was a short-timer, down to the end of his tour, just a few days from home. Streets have corners, you understand, angles, doorways, churchyards, windows, walls to press all that bullshit luck and chance down into sense. Anyway, point being, he called in the coordinates and we waited for air support to come in and solve the problem. That's how we worked it. Get into tight shit and let air support come in close, and then duck down and wait for the napalm heat. We hated them the way you'd hate any savior. They saved your life and took it at the same time, if you know what I mean.'"

"Well, I don't really know what you mean." Merle pounded his stick down. "But I think you should stop right now. I'd venture to say that in this case the redundancy might somehow nullify the jinx. The fact that I've heard this story so many times, and that I find it so boring and even incoherent, and therefore didn't listen to a word you just said, might somehow nudge the odds in our direction."

He shifted through memories in an attempt to locate the original version of Kurt's story, which he'd heard during one of their first afternoons together—still in that honeymoon stage, trading lives with a feverish desire, like lovers in bed— as they sat in what would become their spot near the port, smoking and drinking themselves into a stupor, listening to the roar of the chutes, feeling warm and cozy while the port— whose activity had dwindled down to a trickle in the last few years—suddenly, with the arrival of a ship, seemed grand and substantial. Kurt had explained that the crews on those boats still headed upbound on the Fort William/Port Arthur tack, with top hampers still screaming in the wind, and plates and frames still groaning and flexing against the slush ice blowing in from the east, and their captains still had to contend with the dictates of the Ice Committee of the Lake Carriers' Association, a bunch of business suits in a fancy office in the Rockefeller Building in Cleveland, who gathered bullshit weather reports and used maps and charts and half-assed guesswork to make a call on when the upper lakes could be broken out for the new season.

As Merle had listened to Kurt's talk in those early days, some buried professorial part of himself would rise to the surface as he struggled to make intellectual connections between these ragged memories and his own life. Sitting there with the younger man he could remember what it had felt like lecturing to a class about those souls who—armed with their faith and a hardcore fortitude to put up with natural forces—had risked it all to make a buck, bartering their way along the shore and exploiting the natives one way or another, tapping into the great flex and yaw of capital as it moved between the hinterlands and the cities. A deep knowledge of sequential events, a gloriously full understanding that once allowed him to speak with complete authority, had since fractured to shards— Charlemagne and the Algonquins; Huron villages, bleak and shabby by French standards; Father Jamet; Brother Duplessis; Saint Lalemant; Ennemond Masse—that drifted and cleaved with those from his own personal history: his wife, Emma; his mother-in-law, Gracie; his son, Ronnie; and two dozen men from the Holy Order for People on the Edge Mission, who'd lived out their days before the big, ocular presence of the lake as it pushed against the hardscrabble town, which boom-and-busted its way forward, its grand old homes clutching to the high, terraced land with surprising optimism, seeming to turn a blind eye to the lack of forgiveness in a landscape of mainly stone and ice.

Another time—staggering drunk along Superior Street, holding each other up, arms over shoulders—Kurt had admitted that he didn't see it as a matter of bad luck on Billy-T's part, but rather as bad luck turned to good luck because he'd gotten out of deck duty using Billy-T's death, and it had been rough duty because, approaching Taconite Harbor, the hatches had to be unbolted, ten bolts per hatch, and then he was one of those who'd be lowered down in something called a bosun's chair, nothing more than a slab of wood under your ass and an iron bar coming up through your crotch. They stopped in the middle of the street, face-to-face, and Kurt admitted that Billy-T had most likely lisped the coordinates, and some poor radio operator in forward air control had misheard a number over the net and set the bomb down too close, blowing a few of the men away, including beloved Billy-T himself. The fact that Kurt was able to use the story to get out of deck duty had saved his life because a deck monkey (that's the phrase he'd used, weeping softly) had been killed that night— "And it wasn't me," he said, "it wasn't me. The dock at Taconite is only four feet wide, with a rim of wood along the edge to stop you from sliding, and it was glazed with ice as we came in, and the kid who took my place had done what he was supposed to do, keeping his eye on the line at all times, hauling and hauling, until he went right over the edge."

Then a few weeks ago, walking up to Indian Point Park with nothing to do and no money to spend, just whiling away some hours together, Kurt had admitted that Captain Hopewell hadn't really bought the story he'd told about Billy-T, and had simply been weighing the ramifications of sending a man top-deck who was in such a sorry state of mind. "The salty old bastard was thinking about all the paperwork involved if this stupid deckhand, this shaky kid, were to go overboard. Then they'd have to drop the chains and wait until an official search was made and it would take days, and a few fucking days cut from the manifest would cost the company a fortune," Kurt had said, weeping again. "Captain Hopewell saw that I was just one more goofball 'Nam vet, way over his head when it came to his responsibilities."

•

On the bench, opening his eyes, Merle watched Kurt go down to the shore for a third time, to dip his shoe in the water. It might not matter what either of them said right now, the older man thought. Every big port like this one had a kid just like Kurt, a kid with sea legs on land and land legs at sea, a kid whose life had ended in country, somewhere in the Highlands, or in Khe Sanh, or in Hue, or in Saigon, as a member of Tiger Force, or as a gunner on a Chinook, depending on which version he decided to tell that day. And there was always an old coot whose life had ended in middle age, beginning with a fight over—*over what? he couldn't really remember*—that had resulted in the broken vase (a wedding present), and then another fight and a broken Hitchcock chair (another wedding present), and then another and a broken jaw (*Emma, oh my dear sweet Emma!*). He felt the deep shame of the memory: the clutch of her long, elegant fingers around her chin and her beautiful, deep, sad brown eyes as he'd glanced back one last time before striking out, moving his feet over the ground day after day, until it seemed he'd walked (and he had, for God's sake, he had) the upper shore of Superior, across the border into Canada, and then back down, wending his way to the Hope Mission.

He was on his feet when he came out of it, shaking violently again, leaning all his weight on the handle of his stick.

"You think the ice is coming soon?" he said.

"Christ," Kurt said. "Now you're gonna jinx the fucking ticket. Don't start talking. I heard that one, anyway. Ice, a bet, and a winner. For God's sake."

"I didn't say a word," Merle said.

"You said enough just by asking me if I thought the lake was going to freeze up soon. That's the one *you* drag up every time we scrounge enough to scratch. That's the one *I've* heard a million times."

"I didn't say a word," Merle said. But he wasn't sure because the memory was so strong. The warmth of the mission lounge back when he still had a little bit of his professorial bona fides. Cigar smoke bluing the air, catching the wedge of sunlight as it came through the room, thickening the afternoon while outside in the street the cars hissed through the slush and Jimmy Klein held court in the big leather chair with the split seams along the armrests. An old-timer—at that time—at the mission, his lips cracked and dry from five years of sobriety. Five dry years that had given him a wizened, sharp aspect that made the other men highly uncomfortable.

"You see, the tradition of the ice betting pool goes back a couple hundred years, to when this was a small port," Merle had explained. "Long before supertankers. Back when ships ran on coal and had a beam of something like fifty feet." His voice was strong and authorial. (All the other men in the lounge that afternoon were now dead. Red Jason, an old Iron Range train switchman. Dead. Slappy Jack, a tool-and-die maker with a carbuncle on his neck. Long dead. Jimmy Klein. Long, long, long dead.) The men absently took studious poses, leaning forward with an unusual attentiveness.

"In any event, a man named Frank Lashway, who was about as deep in the drink as you can get, claimed he had a sure bet on when the ice would break. He put down the third day of March and went so far as to say it would break at three in the afternoon. Folks said, 'Lashway, you're sure on that?' and he said, and I quote, 'I'm sure on it. It's not a guess.' Lashway said, 'I got myself a vision on it,' and they said, and I quote, 'You got a drunken vision,' and he said, 'Well, a vision's a vision.' And please understand that all this is factual history; you can find it in the Kitchi Gammi Club archives. They ran the betting pool, at least for upper-class folks, the ship owners and steel mill operators and the like. So a man named Lashway put his bet down on the third day of March."

"Where'd he get the money to bet?" Jimmy Klein had asked. And then Slappy Jack, grunting and moaning, had said, "It don't fucking matter where the wager came from so long as there was a wager in it, you dumb shit, because the point of the professor's story isn't about the amount of the wager; hell, it could've been the shirt on his back for all it matters." And Klein, taking a push, had said, "Hell, it matters how much because without a big wager there's not much to the story at all. He could've been one lucky bastard who pulled a date out his ass with a million other guys pulling dates out their asses and he just happened to hit the nail and so we're hearing the story. Otherwise, he'd've just been lost like the rest of them. So what I'm saying is that the amount of the wager should mean something, because if it was a big one, his house, his wife's house in Wisconsin, something along those lines, then the story goes beyond just a guy with a lucky guess and becomes something else."

He'd gone on like that until, finally, Merle had cleared his throat, stroked his chin, gazed through the smoke, and said, "We shall say he wagered his house, one he hadn't seen in years but knew still existed, on a hundred-acre farm down in Green Bay, and that he wagered a draft horse and a plow and a new gizmo for shucking corn, just for the sake of my story, if that helps, because the wager—and I'm agreeing with your argument, Jimmy—should matter, in theory; so if it helps you to appreciate my story, put a big wager in there. Whatever the case, the third day of March came and it was cold, cold as hell, and the harbor was still jammed, not a hint of thaw, not a hint of breaking up, and so on and so forth. The record indicates, at least as well as I could find, that Lashway went out on the ice. Just about the entire town of Duluth gathered to watch him pick his way over the drifts along the shoreline, and out to the smoother surface beyond. About a quarter mile out, he stopped and began chopping with an ax, just his elbow kipping up and down until there was a crack. Not a boom, but a single, loud, electric snap—you can imagine this, can't you?—and the ice started to break, and of course Lashway was sucked into the water and therefore released from the burden of the wager, so to speak, not knowing if he'd won or lost. And he did win, you see, but he didn't know it, so perhaps theoretically he didn't."

The men had mumbled and grunted, puffed smoke, looked solemnly at the television set. They'd often heard this type of story: preposterously out of tune with reality, but still as true as anything, mirroring their own desperation. ("Any one of us might've done the same," Slappy Jack had said. "You have to admit that, don't you?") It wasn't the image of someone out there on the ice that had struck home. It wasn't the ice breaking up around his boots. They'd all felt such stupefying forces. What resonated through them—as they waited, paused, spat into the spittoon, smoked, watched television, shifted, adjusted cuffs, squeezed balls, flicked bitten fingernails, listened to the clock vibrate by the check-in desk—was all that cash the guy would never collect. Finally Klein had said, "Fix the goddamn set," and got up to twist and fiddle the rabbit ears, spreading them wide; and as he reached around behind to turn the control knob, the picture drew into a tighter screw formation, and the same faces—one after another—rotated over and over, up to the edge of the screen and into eternity.

•

"If I win some cash I'm gonna head back to Benton Harbor and see how things squared away in my absence," Kurt was saying. "And I'm not talking about this penny-ante scratch, but a big payout on a big ticket. Because if we win this one we should go buy a bunch of big-pot tickets. Because if this scratch is a winner it means we did something right, and if we don't make use of that fact it'll just be more of the same." He was speaking from a squatting position and gesturing at the lake, which was now glossy and deep silver in the fading evening light, the color of mercury.

"I believe we should wait a few more minutes," Merle said from the bench. The cold was seeping through his trousers and into his aching knees. "I think we agreed that we wanted to see at least one star appear, or the moon. Some indication that there's something beyond the sky. I think we said that."

"I'm getting too goddamned cold to wait," Kurt said. Then he began talking about a girl he'd known in Chicago, shortly after he'd returned from the war. He'd taken her for a spin along Lake Shore Drive, up to the old fairgrounds, where he found a place to park. Then some punk kids had surrounded the car and broken a bottle on the fender, and he'd gotten out with a crowbar in hand.

He was still talking, but Merle had stopped listening; it was another threadbare story that Kurt told himself day after day after day to get a grip on a postwar rage so tremendous it had seemed mesmerizing.

"You'll come back, won't you?" Merle said. He was struggling to stand again. He wanted to be standing when the kid scratched the ticket.

"How's that?"

"If you go to Benton Harbor, will you come back here?"

Over at the bridge a warning bell began to clang, and the great gears were moving and the weights sliding down, as the span rose for one last ship. They listened to the gurgle of the turning screw and the murmur of the engine and then, a minute later, two woefully long signals from the vessel's horn, announcing its departure.

Kurt winced and took Merle's hand in his own and said, "I'll come back, believe me, you know I will. And anyway, it wouldn't be good luck to say I wouldn't, would it? At least not now, not here."

The ship appeared in the channel, looming over the wall, a giant supertanker—painted gray and white—about the length of a football field. They could hear the slap of wake and the glug of exhaust coming up from the screw.

"That'll be the final one for the season, I'd guess," Merle said.

"You and your ice again," Kurt said. "That boat's a thousand-footer, too long to fit the locks in the St. Lawrence. It's trapped in the lakes." He slapped his hand anxiously against his coat pocket.

"I believe this is the right moment," Merle said. "According to Saint de Brébeuf, or maybe Lalemant, the Huron played a dish game—I think it was called—with five or six fruit stones painted black on one side and white on the other, and they repeated this word *tet* that influenced the play, so maybe you should say 'tet' as you scratch it." He watched the ship leave them behind. "They played for the recovery of the sick, I think. The game was prescribed by a physician, but it was more effective if the sick man requested it."

"Oh, Jesus, if it'll save me from one of your historical lectures, I'll scratch this fucker right now," Kurt said, pulling the ticket—shiny and silvery in the dusky light—from his coat pocket and slapping it against his palm. From his other pocket he took a coin, and then, saying, "tet,

tet,

tet,

tet,

tet,

tet,"

he walked to the water and began to scratch, watching as the numbers appeared one after another. He scratched while the darkening sky—purple dissolving to black—seemed to harden the surface of the lake, and the town, behind them, seethed in the deep silence of loss, another day burned out in the fury of decline. He scratched as if he knew in his heart (and he did, he really did) that within hours the cold air, having gathered itself, would drive down from the plains of Manitoba and Saskatchewan, pound past the Knife River, sweep the length and breadth of the lake with an intensity that would seem a personal affront to both of them, as they lay in their beds and reexamined the afternoon from all sides, wondering what they'd done wrong, and how they could avoid the jinx the next time.

•

Months later, deep in winter, they would go back yet again and deliberate and ponder the moment they'd scratched the ticket. It was all in good fun, reconsidering the past. After all, both men had long since demolished a sense of linear time; it was gone, buried under the losses that had been compiled. But on occasion, in moments of drunk or high hope, they'd take a shot and try to arrange the order of things and make declarations so out of proportion to the realities of their lives that they would trigger fits of mutual hilarity. Merle might say that he was thinking of returning to teaching, that he yearned for the days in front of a class, with all those eager kids leaning into notebooks, scribbling away, taking down every fucking thing he said. Then Kurt might say that he was just going to forget fucking 'Nam and live in the moment, right now, right here, and put all his shit behind him, and Merle would pause for a long, long time—sometimes hours, sometimes days—and, in a highly pontifical voice, with his finger to his chin, he'd say, "The likelihood of you forgetting what happened in 'Nam and seizing the day is about as high as the Huron rising up from the dusty corridors of history and reclaiming their rightful place in the progression of civilization," and then they'd fall into spasms of laughter, kicking the sidewalk with their heels, and Merle would do a crazy, arthritic dance that made him look light on his feet. These were the glorious moments between them, when the burdens of their respective regrets seemed to merge and disappear, and it was because of these purifications that they were still together, still hanging on.

Snow was falling around them. Silence draped the town. The lake was a white shawl beneath a bowl of stars, pure and clear. Kurt had his arms around the old man, helping him walk, and then impulsively pulled him close and felt his frailty, the bones coming up against his skin; and all at once they were aware of the sorry picture the two of them must've made, shuffling through the drifts and hugging to keep warm.

"If we win the next one," Merle said, his voice airy and dry, "I'll find Emma, for good, and apologize and tell her I'm a new man and buy back the land I owned down near the Au Sable, where I was going to build a fishing cabin." And Kurt, without skipping a beat, said, "And I'm going to locate Billy-T's sister, who I always loved, and set her up really good with a house and the works, and see if we can make a life together." Then they heaved out of the drifts and into the center of the road, where the plow had cleared a smooth patch of ice, and began to laugh, falling into routine. It was a clean, open grace that appeared and disappeared with just enough regularity to keep them together, and it would end when the world ended, or perhaps it wouldn't.

THE TREE LINE, KANSAS, 1934

Five days of trading the field glasses and taking turns crawling back into the trees to smoke out of sight. Five days on surveillance, waiting to see if by some chance Carson might return to his uncle's farm. Five days of listening to the young agent, named Barnes, as he recited verbatim from the file: Carson has a propensity to fire warning shots; it has been speculated that Carson's limited vision in his left eye causes his shots to carry to the right of his intended target; impulse control somewhat limited. Five days of listening to Barnes recount the pattern of heists that began down the Texas Panhandle and proceeded north all the way up to Wisconsin, then back down to Kansas, until the trail tangled up in the fumbling ineptitude of the Bureau. For five days, Barnes talked while Lee, older, hard-bitten, nodded and let the boy play out his theories. Five days reduced to a single conversation.

Years later, retired, sitting on his porch looking out at the lake while his wife clanked pots in the kitchen, whistling softly to herself, he'd know, or think he knew, that even at that moment in Kansas, turning to speak to Barnes, he'd had a sense that one day he'd be retired and reflecting on that particular point in time—back near the tree line—because that was what you did after spending much of your career trying to think the way other folks might think. When you retired, you turned back into yourself and tried to settle into not thinking about the way others thought. You rested your feet and sat around tweezing apart past scenarios that had ended up with you alive and others dead, taking advantage of the fact that you were still alive while those others weren't, and in doing so relishing—with a religious sort of glory—the fact that you retained the ability to look out at a lake on a clean, quiet summer day while the wind riffled the far side and a single boat oared gently, dragging a fishing line.

•

Five days he had listened to Barnes, staying quiet, holding back on saying much until that last day, when Barnes turned and said, Look, Lee, all we're doing out here is wasting time. Carson isn't coming. I mean, hell, let's face it, it's unlikely that he's going to arrive down that road. And so Lee said, finally, Well, if Carson comes it'll be because he has weighed the big risk of us being here against an even bigger payoff. As you've pointed out, he's not the type who would come back just to see kinfolk. He's not the type—and, Christ, we've seen enough of those—who would put himself at risk to visit an uncle on a failed farm. If he comes, it'll be to get a stash of loot. No other reason. But for these guys that's good enough. If he's got some loot out here, he'll take the risk. It's that simple. Now I'm going back to have a smoke in the trees and take a break. And without waiting for a response he crawled through the weeds to the trees, where, released from his obligations to the younger agent, he stretched the stiffness out of his legs, lit a cigarette, and felt, for the first time, the tingle deep in his gut as it went to work, zeroing in—as only a gut can zero—on the following particulars:

1. The imperceptibly slow shift of light over the past few days as the dirt-clod shadows stretched across the field and then shortened gradually until, after the sun's zenith, they lengthened while the sky loosened its grip on the sun and a violet, ruddy marl blushed the horizon.

2. The way the road spread out of the vanishing point, exposing its mouth to the farm while, at the same time, tapering back into the quivers of heat in a manner that made it hard, and at times impossible, to watch.

3. The sight of Carson's uncle Vern, coming out on Monday, and again on Thursday, shuffling with a slight hobble, bent-backed, moving around the house and disappearing from sight for a few minutes (causing an uptick of unease in both men as they waited for him to reappear), then backing the tractor out with the plow attached and tilling, it seemed, for the sake of toil itself, because it was clear that the land was dead and worthless. Plowing the same patch on Thursday that he had plowed on Monday, sending up a cloud of dust that hovered in the air.

4. The unseemliness, in an F.B.I. agent, of Barnes's occasional outbursts (Shit, what a waste of time!). Always a phrase or two about the pointlessness of the assignment in relation to the use of time and to things he might otherwise be doing: e.g., tracking that syndicate thug—John Bradfield—whose file, loaded with tips, was tucked in his desk drawer back at headquarters.

5. The gradual broadening of his own awareness of the farm and its connection to the web of cat roads, as they were called, both northwest and southeast, along with even smaller roads whose purpose had been lost to time: old wagon trails and Indian paths that arrayed themselves as potential routes all the way to the outer edges of the Chicago stockyards. (Off-map roads were the bane of the Bureau.) These cat roads had started to impress themselves on Lee's awareness during drives back to town, passing gaps in the fence line where they emerged out of the grass. On Monday, Barnes said, So far as I can see, he has one way in, and one way out. Which would make Carson even more of a fool if he tried to come here to visit. On Tuesday, he said, This is a trap. One way in, one way out. He's not the type to play into a trap. (That's the way it worked: An inexperienced young agent often restated what he thought was obvious about the setup, repeated the known details again and again, as if to assure himself that everything was positioned correctly, that what

had been imagined in the Chicago office—using maps and line drawings—properly matched the Kansas reality.)

6. A flaw inherent in the dynamic between the two partners as they lay side by side, staying as still as possible while the weeds—mostly wild oat grass, with a patch of Queen Anne's lace—shifted, languorously translating the breeze on Wednesday (the only day with wind) into motion, as if the world, unfurling itself with stunning elegance, were preparing for the imminent arrival of God, or gun, his gut told him, in those exact words. Something big was coming, the wind had said. It was a sure giveaway. Any experienced lawman knew that the wind rising like that had to mean something. But Lee had been distracted by the kid. After all, you read the landscape for signs: the way a road stays quiet for a certain amount of time; a lonely weed patch in the Four Corners region that, after three days of relative calm, is suddenly darkened by one of those odd cloud formations, not a thunderhead but a cloud that seems to refuse to achieve its full growth, giving you, as you sit in the car chewing a toothpick, a sense that something is amiss.

7. It wasn't simply what Barnes said, or his awkward inability to establish any kind of mature silence, but also the way he rounded his words, polishing them up, buffing them into a style of elocution

that clashed with the landscape. He spoke with the sucked-in-cheeks manner of a man holding forth with unearned authority, as he said: It's highly unlikely, Lee, regarding the patterns set forth by his previous movements, that he would alas venture, as I've said a few times before, to risk arriving at a location known to fit into his past movements. Snapping off his clean white teeth, his voice had a gee-whiz youthfulness until, catching hold, it shifted to take on the hardscrabble surroundings. Then he tightened in his phrases and tried as best he could to sound world-weary (never looking at Lee at those moments; turning away from Lee's eyes, flecked gray, crinkled and set deep in the folds of his face, old-Texas-lawman style), saying, Here's how I see it, sir: Carson started out a phony. Just another kid trying to make a name for himself as a stickup man. No real heart. He tried to look the Robin Hood part by handing over some cash to a few clodhopper bank customers. But by the time he got north he had too much heat. Now he has that shoot-first style that comes out of knowing the truth. If you know the truth, you shoot first. At that point, Barnes's voice shifted again, sliding naturally into the rut of his thoughts, opening up to a deeper, more speculative tone as he droned on and on (or so it seemed to Lee, who kept his eyes on the farm), explaining how Carson was a man with a sense of self, who knew who he was in a way the old yeggs didn't. Carson operated out of a deeper psychology, playing himself

off what he knew others were thinking, not only
playing the patterns of the law, which were usually
pretty easy to figure out, but also what the law,
most likely, would speculate; so that it was unlikely, say, that he'd come back around—even if
there *was* loot involved—to dig something up at
his uncle's farm, knowing instinctually that we
would have it covered . . . (Lee half listened, trying
to blank out the kid's voice, focusing his attention
away from the house and onto the road, which
came in straight from the horizon. The horizon,
he understood, was a foe. The horizon altered
the odds. The horizon—always mesmerizing if
stared at too long—might take over the stakeout.
Lee had once been beaten by the horizon in
Waco, working freelance for the governor, tracking a killer named Newfield. Two days staking
out a shack until his eyes lingered too long on
the horizon—twilight—and got stuck there while
his prey took advantage and, before Lee could
shake himself awake, roared off in a rooster tail of
dust.) Barnes was still talking, saying, This guy
knows we're looking for patterns, and he's even
considered, I'd venture to say, the idea that we'd
expect him not to come back here, and in expecting him to expect us to expect him not to come
back, he'd expect that we'd take that expectation
into consideration—the potential pattern—and
stake out his old uncle's farm. You see, Lee, I think
he has a self-awareness that a man like Hoover
doesn't. (And *you* do, Lee thought, lifting his head,

nodding, feeling—again—an intense hankering
for a cigarette.)

Years later at his summer cottage in Wisconsin, sitting on the
porch and staring out at the water, listening to Emma inside
cooking or watching television, he'd go back to that conversation, holding it out for examination, and wonder if he had mis-
stepped at that point. Shut your yap, he might have said. Clam
up, kid. You can talk until you're out of words, but, no
matter what you might say or think, the fact that there is a
chance Carson might show is the only thing that matters.
Even later, Lee would understand that by holding back on
his side of the argument he had allowed for a much more dangerous distraction, a paternal vibration—unsettling and
unspoken—between the two of them. (That kid was like a son
to me, he told his wife. He annoyed me the way I used to an-
noy my old man. Except the old man would've boxed my
ears off.)

That afternoon, as he crawled back to Barnes, the gut feeling worked its way up his throat and struggled into his
head. Note: A gut feeling finally becomes a hunch when it is
transmuted into the form of clear, precise verbal statements
uttered aloud to a receptive listener—internal or external—
who responds in kind. A hunch twists inside the sinews and
bones, integrating itself into the physicality of the moment,
whereas a gut feeling can only struggle to become a hunch,
and, once it does, is recognized in retrospect as a gut feeling.
Before Lee could express his hunch, Barnes wiped his brow
with his handkerchief and said, Jesus, Lee, where'd you go?
Into town for a bite? And Lee said, No, just a smoke. Anything
happening out there? Barnes raised the field glasses, lowered

them, pursed his lips as if in deep thought, and then said, in a newly formed sarcastic voice, Hell, you missed the whole thing, Lee. Carson came rolling up with the entire gang. I think Pretty Boy Floyd was along for the ride. Women and all. They had a picnic over there by the windmill—fried chicken, watermelon, apple pie, the works. Shot a few guns into the air in celebration, dug up the loot (you were right about that), and took off. I let them, on account of you not being here. I said to myself, Agent Lee's smoking a few back there and I'm not inclined to bother the man. Now, if you don't mind, I'm going to go back and have a cigarette myself. Then he crawled off through the weeds and disappeared into the trees, leaving Lee alone to watch the farm.

·

Fate operates retroactively. By trading smoking breaks, the two men had tried to wedge apart the tedium as well as they could, breaking the days up, sustaining attention on the field and house according to the dictates of training, knowing that at least one of them had to keep his eyes fixed on the farm, because if they both looked away, even for a minute, it would in theory betray Agent Jones and Agent Tate, who had drawn the night watch, drinking coffee from a vacuum flask, nudging each other awake, coming out to the road in the morning, bone-tired, saying, Nothing moved out there, not even the darkness. Not a damn thing, a total zero. Good luck, boys.

·

Years later, in the reductive, slowed-down replay of memory, the Buick sedan—stolen fresh off a lot in Topeka—appeared suddenly, having come in off a cat road that ran west and hit the main road a quarter mile from the Carson farm, deep enough in the quivering heat to provide the element of surprise. First, just a glint of chrome radiator, a spark of light where the road bled itself into plowed field. Then, in a matter of seconds, the glint turned into a full-blown automobile, swinging alongside the house, roaring to a stop, rocking heavily as it disgorged three men. (Lee used the word in his report, saying, The car disgorged three men, who spread out to reconnoiter the homestead.) Carson appeared a moment later, stepping from the car with his hands spread wide, limping slightly (the Michigan City ricochet wound, festering), glancing around nervously as he directed the men while Lee, hidden in the grass, instantly understood the following:

A. Four years of heists and encounters with law enforcement had given Carson's men an innate sense that certain probabilities—a stakeout, limited to two or three men—were best dealt with in a swift, heedless manner that included overwhelming firepower brought to bear on weary Bureau men who most likely had been in surveillance mode for days, hiding themselves in the grass or behind trees. (They knew we were there, Lee said later. They figured we'd be one, maybe two at the most. We were shorthanded and they understood that fact. I froze up. My judgment regarding how much field was between my position and the house was skewed. I was alone. Outgunned.)

B. As Carson's men charged forward, they felt keenly, albeit intuitively, the way surveillance compressed time, tightening it in—days of inaction punctuated only by occasional shit breaks, piss breaks, smoke breaks and drink breaks, food breaks and stretch breaks interrupted only by small, inconsequential peripheral actions observed. (City men came into a farm scene like fire through ice, Lee would think later. They had that city jaunt, whereas we had forgotten the way time worked outside the confinement of the farm.)

C. Carson's men strode ahead, as if through the streets of Chicago, their black suit coats even blacker in the hazy light. They had an elegant disregard for the landscape that came from the fact that most of them had been born and raised on farms or in dusty small towns, and had pushed that part of their lives behind them, learning how to stand in the city, adjusting cuffs, snapping hat brims, touching ties while shrouding their true intentions in wisecracks, moving around constantly in order to belie the static silence of the scene at hand. While the men closed in on Lee's position, Carson stepped slowly to the right of the barn, looking down at his feet, moving, despite his slight limp, with an ease that bespoke his desire, even in this setting, to look casual, lifting his head to sniff the air before continuing along the side of the house. (He started at the southern end of the house, put one foot in front of the other,

heel to toe, marking carefully, trying to locate the
spot where the loot was buried, Lee would write
in his report.)

·

Back in the tree line, Barnes had smoked two cigarettes while
he took in the view: a slight glen in the trees formed by the
creek, rimmed by a small fringe of green fern. The horizon
was mercifully lost in the trees, so from that vantage—factoring
in his profound sense that the stakeout was futile—it was likely
that he felt a deeper relaxation settle in, an all-knowing sense
of calm that came from being young and inexperienced, and
it was probably this, combined with the pleasure the smoke
was giving him, that led him to think that the moment at hand
was somehow reflective of the general state of the world. (Far
off, the sound of a car engine devoured by land. Far off, a muffled car-door slam.) Whatever had been acting on Barnes's
gut over the several days of the stakeout combined with the
quiet beauty back there, amplified by the barrenness of the
farm in relation to the humiliation (yes, a stakeout was an act
of humility that could easily, if not approached properly, turn
to humiliation), had, in turn, combined with a natural desire
in the young agent and caused him to break free from standard operating procedure, to move naturally, so that the kid
walked out of the tree line that day standing straight and tall,
moving with a sure manner, trusting his gut, struggling ahead
of his own awareness (dulled, Lee would later imagine, by the
persistent tedium of a scene that had gone on, with the exception of the old man plowing on Monday, and again on Thursday, and the wind on Wednesday, for what had seemed, to his
youthful mind, an eternity). He stepped forward into a single,

ferocious moment. He stepped forward into a fury of gunfire while his mind—young and foolish but beautiful nonetheless—remained partly back in the woods, taking in the solitude, pondering the way the future felt when a man was rooted to one place, waiting for an unlikely outcome, one that, rest assured, would never, ever arrive.

CARVER & COBAIN

A few years ago, I drafted two linked stories, one about Kurt Cobain and the other about Raymond Carver. Both grew up in the Pacific Northwest. Both had fathers who worked at a saw-mill. Both were, in one way or another, working-class kids. There was another overlap that I struggled to show, but which was much deeper and had to do with the fact that both struggled with addiction—Carver with drinking, Cobain with her-oin. Cobain in a hotel room that seemed straight out of one of Carver's stories, at least in theory, the details being somewhat fuzzy. The stories sat in a folder and waited for revisions, and I vowed to go back to them together, united. I met Carver one time, when he gave a reading for PEN on the Upper West Side of Manhattan. I told him how much his work meant to me and he thanked me and gave me a nod and a sidelong look—he was smoking, I think, and he took the cigarette out of his mouth and tapped it into the ashtray and then looked past me, over my shoul-der, and I moved to the side and let the next admirer step up. Co-bain was around nineteen when that moment transpired—that must've been sometime around 1986? I imagine Cobain, lonely in a good way, with the smell of pine sap in the air, listening to records and making sketches in his sketchbook, unaware that he and his mother were living inside a Carver story. Perhaps that's a stretch. I would've explained to Carver, if I could have, that when I bought his book of stories, What We Talk About When We Talk About Love, *I began to read and was stunned to recognize the landscape, to see that the world I knew could exist in the world of fiction. In Michigan, my neighbor— Mr. Bycroff, now dead—had worked at the paper mill, the Bryant Mill, just down the hill to the east of my house. He was an electrician in the mill, and he came home in overalls— name patch, tool belt, black lunch pail, the works—and drank by himself on the front porch of his house, and in the night, usually late, from my window I heard him singing to himself, singsong slurred chants, and then, on some occasions, he gave out a kind of howl, or began shouting at his wife, and I heard then but didn't know I was hearing something that I would hear, years later, in Cobain's voice, somewhere around the edges of his singing, pushing as hard as he could to the very edge of a scream yet still, somehow, for me at least, stark and brutally clear and well-wrought.*

CARVER

Years later, he could still recall the way his father had uttered the phrase "coffin nail," waving a cigarette during an argument, and he'd try to tweeze that moment apart, to remember what fury had driven him out of the house that day, down the road, along the side of the overpass to the trail and to the river where the water deepened as it entered the concrete sluice and provided a nice, cool resting spot for fish in the afternoon flow.

One more boy finding solace in the act of fishing while cars went past, dusty and quick, on the road overhead.

Years later, when he was living in Port Angeles, he'd remember that moment and he'd consider his own imminent death—a fact that sat just over the horizon—while upstairs, in the window, the sound of typing came in the air along with a zip sound whenever she, his lover, Tess, returned the platen at the end of a line. It was a sound that told him she was making a poem, cutting the lines sharply against the white edge of the page. It was a soothing and strangely assuring sound that attested to the fact that they had found, he thought, some comfortable mutual arrangement in which to work. With this in mind, he turned back to the memory of that afternoon, and tried once again to find something in it, to locate what he needed: a clear, concise awareness of what had transpired at that moment, far back in time, and in that awareness some elemental image that might be used: the way the hook sometimes caught his shirttail when he brought it up for bait. The corrugation of riffles around a submerged branch. The sound of tires making way on the concrete overpass. The sun as it spread down through the water into the depths and then became darker as it neared the bottom. The softness of the bank, fern and moss and leaf matter as he trod as close as possible without going in, because at that spot the bank gave way clean and sudden into the water. Or, perhaps, going back to the fight: his father's thick calloused hands—nicked and bandaged from saw-blade work at the mill? He tried for a while and then put his pen down and looked out at the sky, milky over the sharp pines, and he remembered the way—one night, maybe when he was sixteen—he'd gone out and looked up at the stars and pondered the clear, hard clarity of eternity . . . and then, on the deck, he thought, not another story with fishing, not another story about a boy and his father and turning to the motions of the cast in the end, to bring it to a close, and then he stopped thinking and listened, again, to the tap of the typewriter keys upstairs where she was, from the sound of it, still writing a poem, breaking the lines. He looked up at the window and then out at the trees again and thought, I'm done with stories, most likely, the last one finished, the one about Chekhov, because each one takes a toll, requires a certain energy, which was limited from the start, even back when I had youthful energy, and each one, the ones that worked, gave me a little bit of fuel to write the next, but now all I get are small bursts, hardly enough for a poem. Once I drew stories out of the chaos and void the same way I reached under the mattress that time, in what I called a drying-out joint, to find my clandestine cigarettes, the pack crumpled and soft, and against the rules smoked at the window, staring out at the sky, feeling the relief and rush of the nicotine. Much later I used some of that in a story, ordered it and gave it some sense when, in truth, it hadn't had much when it was happening, although I'd known, somehow, in that way all writers probably know, that I'd get something out of it eventually, when my life found whatever form of stability was necessary to go on with the work. Upstairs in the window he heard another short burst of typing and he thought, hearing it, that if he could somehow find the energy he'd write the coffin nail story, whatever it might be, as a last gesture to eternity, and put in it the sweet resinous smell of the pine grove and how it felt to wade barefoot over to where the stream smoothed out before going under the road, into that dark sluice, and the risk of being cut by one of the bottles that got tossed out from cars, and he'd go into great detail on the catch he had made that afternoon, having forgotten his net on his rush out of the house, bringing each fish in carefully so as not to lose it. But then, on the deck, coming up and out of the reverie again, he knew that he was only thinking wishfully and that it would not be possible in his weak condition to find the strength to finish one more, and that his work would have to stand on its own, as it was, and that it didn't matter because one couldn't know how one would stand in the future because there was no way to answer that imponderable question that stood in front of you each day of your life, a question that had arrived even before he wrote fiction. He knew that it was impossible because it took a paradoxically light kind of energy to get to that place. It took a kind of power that no longer resided in his limbs. He should not think about how his work would be regarded years from now, in the scheme of things, and if this work would be read. That was the great, imponderable question. It had been there each day of his life. Even before he began to write he had pondered, what will I do or not do to put my mark on the world? It made him think of the Jack London story. Jack goes into a house and begs a meal when he's on the road, talking his way into a woman's kitchen. (This was in his unknown memoir, *The Road*. He had read a stiff-spined old copy at the library one afternoon when he was sixteen, skipping school. He had kept his head down under his coat, like a sleeping bum, to avoid being seen.) London had gone into a kitchen and sweet-talked a meal with a tale about his life. He made up a story to touch the woman's heart. His father had suffered from falling sickness, he told the woman. We were crossing the street and he simply fell down. Then he embellished further and created a dead mother for himself, ranging the countryside for work: from a ranch in Texas to book canvassing and then San Francisco.

Then London added some more woes. He had gone in deep and unfolded his predicament step by step until he had spent long windy nights on San Francisco streets. Meanwhile, the woman fed him biscuits, bacon, and eggs. The key to the story, Carver thought (he had since reread it), lay in the fact that sitting at the table was the woman's son, who was injured, his head bandaged, and who had gazed upon him with wide eyes. In the end, the woman made a bagged lunch for London to take, with hard-boiled eggs, an apple, and even a pair of new wool socks. In the book London wrote: "I hope that woman in Reno will read these lines and forgive my gracelessness and unveracity. I do not apologize, for I am unashamed. It was youth, delight in life, zest for experience, that brought me to her door. It did me good. It taught me the intrinsic kindliness of human nature. I hope it did her good." Back then, he had wondered if he, too, might touch the mind of some soul that way, work himself into the trickery of storytelling. There had been photos in the book—he now remembered—of a man hopping a freight train, leaning off a boxcar, showing some particular technique on how it was done. A part of the book had been about the maneuvering around train cars and the technique involved in evading the yard cops. He thought about that—looking off at the trees and the bright blue sky that had, as of late, become suddenly acutely vivid—and he thought about his own father, who had jumped freights on his way to look for work down in Texas. Not for glory or dreams of fame but simply in search of steady employment, a good job to make ends meet. His father didn't make stories of himself, didn't see himself in that light. He moved in a different kind of water. Yet he might be wrong about that. What could one man know about the inside of another without making something up?

Upstairs, from the window, came the sound of typing, the keys hitting the platen. A rattle of it and then silence, and then some more and then silence again. Yes, his lover was writing a poem, tearing into it, breaking those lines. When he turned back to look at the view, he got a sense, clear and firm, of the story he would write if he had the energy to do so, and the will, the sense not to think too much. It had been in his mind for years, something close to the vest, a part of family history. The time his former wife—as he sometimes thought of her now—had given birth to his daughter, in a hospital back in Yakima. By pure chance his father had been right down the hall in his own ward, working out the demons in his mind, gaunt and thin and barely alive, a man who had been sucked dry of all life. He had gone out in the hall for a cigarette, to take a breather away from the newborn baby, and standing out there he had remembered something: his father beside him on the North Coast Limited. They were passing over the Cascade Range, on the way from Yakima to Seattle, where they were to stay at the Vance Hotel and eat at the Dinner Bell Café. His father had taken a couple of days off from the mill to go on the trip. He had looked out the window and pointed out the sights, using his cigarette as a pointer. Perhaps it had been on that trip that he had first heard the phrase "coffin nail." He wasn't sure. But he knew for sure that he had stood in the hospital hall and thought about the trip and about his father and about the hardships the old man had endured, one after another, in the struggle to make ends meet for the sake of his family. In that image there was the material for some kind of story, a kernel, yet to be created. A wife's glowing, exalted face, and the baby, swaddled tightly in a white cotton blanket as he sleeps the first soft sleep of his life while not far away, just down the white corridors—antiseptic and clean—the baby's grandfather, an old saw sharpener, his hands gnarled and scarred from work, struggled mightily to sort the demonic world from the real world, to get things straight.

Outside the hospital, as he might imagine it, a misty rain would fall, the kind you found in the Pacific Northwest. It would fall—in his story—with a light persistence, as if unwilling to ever ease up, while through the clouds far to the west would be a dull sun, attempting to work its way through the mist. He looked out and thought, If I had the time, I'd write that one. It would certainly be my last, he thought, trying not to cough, feeling his ribs and his chest ache. If he coughed now he would never stop and his love would have to break off from her work upstairs and come down to help. Are you all right, she would say, and he would say, I'm fine, and gather his breath, easing up under her touch. And she would say, What were you thinking about out here, Ray? And he would have to keep it simple. He would have to say, I was thinking about Chekhov. I was thinking about the master.

COBAIN

Alone on a bed in the sad karma of the Crest Motel, or the Marco Polo, take your pick, one last stop on the road through—no, he didn't think anything like that because his mind is impenetrable, untraceable step by step through those last movements, which much later would become legend partly because only he knew where he went those last few days, before returning to the house and the gun. One more guy checks in, waiting to shoot up, with the old fear of needles gone. A connection named Hobert, or Rudy, or Blake out in the parking lot, leaning against his car, glancing up and down for cops, while inside the room he parts the curtains and looks out and then sits back down on the bed, shaking slightly. The room is shabby with wood paneling and has that reek (*The sky an excrement beneath our feet!*), having served fifty years of trysts: lovers cusped by the sagging springs into the dead center of the bed. (There was that time in Vegas, that fuckup of a weekend when the glitter and gloss of the future was just ahead and everything became reduced to beautiful impulse, the drive into art, or so it seemed, and in that moment everything hugged reality, the actuality of time doubling back on itself. At that time still living near Aberdeen, sur-rounded by logging detritus, not only the trees, but the old mills, too, the shabby ransacked vestiges of the lumber age, timber thrust into the bite of the blade, halved and halved again into board feet.) On the bed he might be thinking about the times his father took him to the mill. The time his mother and father fought and his mother ended up alone on the couch, face in hands, saying, "It's over, over, over," and he left her there and went outside to walk alone through the cold, pine-tree night, the smell of sap and wood smoke, and then he stopped to look up through the branches at the stars, far up, a firmament in the great bowl of cosmos and then—and this was when, he admits (secretly), apparent only in the re-ductio ad absurdum of introspection—he felt destiny for the first time: a keen awareness that he would someday, some-how, prevail and obtain, almost against his will, the fame and stardom that has—he likes to think, although he knows it's simplistic bullshit—driven him here to the Crest, or maybe it's the Quest Hotel, to satisfy the need of his bones.

He goes to the window and parts the curtain and lights a

smoke and draws deeply as he watches his connection in the parking lot who, in turn, is watching him, glancing his way and nodding slightly.

There was an evidentiary moment, place, connector, or apex when his longing to create and to be heard and known met up with something else (insecurity, self-loathing, take your pick) and turned in on itself so that, to survive it, he had to go back and reclaim what was lost, and in doing so remembered the past.

(How does one make a story out of the enigmatic non-stuff of self-immolation, out of the death impulse, when the will to live, bright small compact lifeblood, of baby lift, hefting the child up to hear the chortling, the bloody first giggle, gives way to the urge to avoid procreation, to find some terminal point? For God's sake, all one can do is make raw conjecture.)

Back on the bed, watching the curtain shake, he knows that this is what will form around him, in the end.

(Maybe that's part of the deal. He longs for a hazy non-narrative around whatever he has left of his own story. But then, maybe not. Maybe it's just a reduction of the mental into the physical. Anybody who has suffered addiction knows the story, and anyone who has suffered chronic pain can under-stand the moment at hand.)

On the bed he's humming softly. In theory, he has another song to write, one more fragment to put to tape. All he has is a fragment of melody with a few words—Hamlet/fuckin/dimwit—and not much else, but he's humming it as he remem-bers a time his mother took him to Seattle, cutting alongside Capitol State Forest, and he had leaned his cheek against the cold car window while she pointed to the mountain and explained to him how a tree line forms, up in the higher reaches where the oxygen thins and it's snowy all year, and he followed her finger up to the peaks and felt a distinctive sense, maybe for the first time, of being able to see, really see, in a secretive way, the inside of the world, and in the car that day he thought to himself: I'll remember this moment, even when I'm an old fuck, and then looking over at his mother, dressed in capri pants and a white blouse, her Ray-Bans on, a kerchief over her hair, he straightened himself up and imagined himself as a man, as a father, and then he yelled yeeee hoooo, at the top of his lungs.

TWO RUMINATIONS ON
A HOMELESS BROTHER

SVIATOSLAV RICHTER

There's this old man who walks along the fence next to the hospital, or, say, down near town, wobbling in his loose, flapping shoes, digging around in the garbage can on the corner, smoking a cigarette, clutching it between his battered fingers, or simply walking with his shoulders braced as if he knows he is some kind of fodder for speculation, because it seems to be so consistent, his homeless rooting, keeping to a pattern, moving south on Midland Avenue for a half mile to Franklin Place and then left on Franklin and down Franklin to River Road, along River Road to Front Street, left on Front and up Front back to Midland, and then, presumably, around again. By virtue of his consistency, he has edged his way into the consciousness of just about everybody who has driven more than once down Midland Avenue, or Front Street, or, to a lesser degree, Franklin Place.

Rain or shine, for about a year and a half, give or take, he has slogged with the same gimp, the same loping swing of arms, the same cigarette burning between his fingers, and he's rooted in the same trash cans—the one on the corner of

Midland and Franklin, or the one on the corner of River and
Front. Leaning down with his underwear showing in winter,
pale yellow, say, or his pants hiked up too far over his shirt in
summer, he goes against the elemental facts in a disconcert-
ing way that makes those passing him shrug and wonder
briefly what his story might be before going back to their
lives, half caring and half not caring, subsumed in the responsibilities at hand, so to speak, or caring deeply with a flash
of intense sadness and wonder, resolving to sign up to work
at the shelter in town, the Soup Haven, or whatever it's called,
or not caring one iota and getting riled up thinking about the
ease with which a man can pass his life in what must be a
pleasurable vortex of non-time that comes from following a
set path day after day, say, insane or on the edge of insanity,
as a way of escaping responsibilities, dodging them for the
poetic stance of being the odd homeless gent, strangely formal in the way he daintily roots, poking at the trash with a
stick, his face like that of an old sea captain, say, or of a farm-
hand of some type, which leads some to speculate that he was
once one of those ship workers, river pilots who at times come
in to land at the dock on the river to catch a cab down to the
Bronx, expounding stories of bridge heights and the way the
tides have to be calculated before you take a ship upriver, at-
testing to the way it all works—one man captaining the boat
from the harbor to the river mouth, another bringing it upriver.
Weather-beaten, some think while passing him on a windy day,
watching the way he lists with his arms out at his sides, wing-
like, the tail of his shirt fluttering behind him as he walks.

The way he roots through the garbage cans in the winter
snow and in the summer heat with an admirable persistence
serves as a touchstone, fueled by the concept of mental illness

afloat over the land, even, say, for the less educated observers who just see him and think, Fucking crazy old homeless bastard hanging in there, still going, still doing his thing. The phrase "mental illness" shrouds his body as he walks, and orients him, slips him like a peg into whatever dreamy ideas of madness fill the minds of those passing and pushes away the thought that he is, in a way, say, a reflection of some part of themselves that might, someday, under the right circumstances—a financial loss leading to ruin, say, or some neurological disorder, an improper linking of nerves, or a shady haze of undetected tumor, or some sharp trauma abrupt enough to throw off their general balance—irrevocably force them into the same circumstances, wandering day after day, sticking to the same general pattern, stopping to dig in the public trash can for discarded bottles or scraps of food or newspapers to read.

Those who pass have had a sense that perhaps, at least in theory, at least as some kind of innate potential, they may—unlikely, hugely unlikely—someday find themselves in the same circumstances, although with variations, of course, find themselves feeling something that isn't simply shame but something deeper in the self, an obliviousness that allows for wandering in ice-cold air with your shirt wide open, a deprivation of life force, or of gumption, or of will that could leave you shuffling through a limited space, say, always keeping close to the safety of shelter if there is shelter, or to the house of older parents who, bewildered by the state of your life, will take you in and give you a bed and care for you as best they can, telling you to stay in when it's cold, building a fire, listening and waiting for you to speak with coherence, to give a sign that somehow you are going to pull out of this and get your life back together, say, or that you are just gathering your equilibrium and finding a foothold in reality, or at least in common sense, having known you—your parents—when you were a full-blown functioning adult in the world, making deals, establishing relationships with others, cleaning your body and dressing in accordance with the climatic conditions, enjoying good days and bad days, lingering over the beauty of the world, over, say, an amazingly graceful football play in which the receiver hooks his arm up without looking to clutch the ball in a way that seems to defy not only the nature of physics itself but something more, the potential in the act itself, or, better yet, over, say, the way a kid, like your own son or daughter, if you have one, looks up at you, beaming after accomplishing some new task, such as putting a round peg into a round hole instead of a square one, or, even better, over, say, the way the pianist Sviatoslav Richter occasionally held back from playing while the audience waited and grew impatient, first making noise, mumbling and talking, anxious and expectant, while he sat on the bench and held his fingers poised to play, letting the sound of the Moscow hall reverberate with all the coughing and tense laughter, the whispering, and then waited and waited until a deep quiet fell, a silence that anticipated the first notes and then grew even deeper, it was said, until there was nothing but the creak of the seats and the soft, muted thump of shoe soles against wooden floorboards, and then an even deeper, astonished silence that seemed, in all its starkness, accusatory and frank, judging the ineptitude of those who would, in a few minutes—or by that point perhaps never—listen to the beautiful music that his fingers would produce if they received the proper instruction from the brain of the virtuoso, who was temperamental and elegant and oddly dumb at the same time, a man holding his fingers clawed over the keys and casting back upon the world an innate sense of that which lies between the flesh and the soul, forcing it on the audience with his unusual—albeit par for the course when it comes to creative geniuses—behavior.

OH, ROCKLAND!

It's not just that you went to visit him when he was in Rockland, now called Blaisdell Addiction Treatment Center, stopping on the way to pick up some hard candies and a bagel and a large coffee, as he had requested, and that you went and checked in with the receptionist and signed the register and ignored (as best you could) her blunt, bored stare from the other side of the window—the grille of the voice-hole mute and silent—and then went through what seemed like a set of air-lock doors to the elevator, standing alongside one or two other visitors who also held bags of food, and then went up to attend the obligatory class, hearing the same nurse give the same speech about FREEDOM (Focus on thought; Remember where it leads; Eliminate the error; Explore other options; Don't react, respond; Organize thoughts; Motivate to do better), her face slack and sweet but also bored, everyone uncomfortable on the hard steel chairs, with the sense that through the door the patients were gathering, waiting.

It's not just that you drove over there and parked and felt the sorrow of the locked ward from the outside—the building relatively new on the old hospital grounds, the other buildings, some barracks-like, others elegant and Gothic, their windows boarded up with blank sheets of plywood, mildewed gray, gaping—knowing that you'd enter his building and go through the abovementioned routine, also aware as you sat in the car for a minute that the same hospital had a mention in the Ginsberg poem, again and again ("I'm with you in Rockland!"), which made you feel part of literary history somehow, and also made you wonder if perhaps you could use this in a story, take advantage of the fact that you were in a real situation with your real brother, who was back again in what might be the terminal treatment for his condition.

It's not just that the third time you visited him you sat in the car and rehashed the way it would happen, at least until you got in and sat with him face-to-face, listening to whatever he was going to say, sharing the food, leaning back, taking in the room—the little kids visiting fathers, the older folks visiting young patients, the celebratory hilarity of the homecomings lifting the air with a sweet vibration—sat in the car and rehashed the way you'd go in, face the mute receptionist, go through the air-lock device, and then sit through the talk on FREEDOM again, after checking your food bag with the orderly. It's not just that the third time you went to visit, on an autumnal day with the leaves brilliant in the sharp morning sunlight, you'd go through the routine and then sense again, while you were talking, trying to coax him into a positive vision of what he might become, the cycle of the entire story up to that point, rolling in hoops, swinging around both of you, and you'd shrug it off and watch while your brother removed the lid of his cup, blew across the surface, and took a sip and then another sip and then leaned his head back and swallowed, flexing his throat and the sinewy muscles of his neck, exposing his gaunt breastbone, which looked covered in tissue paper, and then, when his head came back down, met your gaze with deep brown eyes while between you, in the quiet, unspoken silence that suddenly opened, there would be such a thick exchange of information that you'd both tear up and clear your throats and you'd push the bag forward and say, I brought you a bagel, like you asked, and some hard candies, and he'd give you a look that was so thankful, so absurdly out of proportion to your act of kindness that you would know right there—amid the din of love talk between visitors and patients—that the tenor of his thank-you would come back to haunt you later, no matter what happened.

It's not just that in the car before going up on the third visit you'd granted yourself a bitter kind of solace, because you were not locked up there and he was, and you were able to find words to situate yourself in life, and he didn't seem able to do so at that moment—a kind of purity of resolve (in the car) that sat behind your eyelids when you shut your eyes and let the sunlight purge through in a blood burst of warm red. It's not just the clean, hard facts that you understood, in the car, and that were so threadbare and old hat that almost anyone could have recited them, beginning with the use of chemicals that sparked dopamine production and lodged themselves in organic compounds called receptors, and then from there took over what was originally a unique story—the Hudson River house, the artwork, his stone-carved faces in the front yard, the view of the river from his back patio, his name, Frank, the minutiae of his story—and transmuted it into a clichéd tale that changed only in the terms that were used to describe it, so that those who were once known as mad, Skid Row bums, stumblebums and drunkards and junkies, were now seen as diseased victims who might be treated.

It's not just the fact that in the car, or a few minutes later, riding up in the elevator with an older couple who told you they were from the Bronx, both working people, you were aware that part of the tragedy of the situation was the loss of story inherent in the hospital walls, the sealed doors, the sign-in sheet, and the folding chairs that were standard issue for this sort of place, along with the social worker who had a heavy

Haitian accent and told you, when you were done with the visit, that he'd watch out for your brother in particular, responding to your politeness (you were extra polite), his face wide, moonlike, and his eyes watery, at his place behind the nurse's desk outside the meeting room. It's not just the way he told you that your brother stood out as a lively patient, that he was getting his act together, and that he would, quote, soon find his path, he likes to draw and everyone knows he's an artist, unquote.

It's not just that you went home and read Thomas Merton and reread a line you'd underlined in his book *Seeds of Contemplation*, which stated in no uncertain terms that humility was the only antidote to despair—that you read it a few times and then went into a deep contemplation out on your back deck, smoking a cigar, wondering if there was a way to become humble before the preordained humiliation of a chemical addiction, wondering if the narrative thrown around your brother would look just as absurd when folks in the future found out that it had nothing at all to do with the way the compounds locked into receptors but originated with something else that was, at that time, out on the deck, out in the world, as mysterious to you as it was to everyone else.

It's not just that he went from a halfway house called Open Arms, a neat and tidy little house in the town of Haverstraw, tucked up amid the river-town streets, with a view of the river—a glint of blue through the trees in the summer, more stark and open in the winter—to the hospital cleanup ward, and then up to Rockland for the first time, and then back to Open Arms again for a second stay, and then back to the emergency-room cleanup ward, and then up to Rockland (as you'd think of it some of the time), and then out of Blaze (as you began to call it later) into Open Arms again, and then to Blaze for a third, final time, which seemed to matter so much the third time you went to visit him, sitting in the car, watching the rain come down, the smell of the bagel and the coffee in the air, ruminating over the way the names of the institutions seemed to map out with neat concision, to make orderly what wasn't orderly, as if language itself were straining to show in clear terms the structure of the story that was forming around him, just as his wife's name had matched the name of his first roommate in the halfway house, and he had felt the mockery of fate itself, had said to you, Jesus, what are the chances that I'd have a roommate with a slightly feminine name and a wife with a slightly masculine name, and that somehow I'd be put in with this guy who is half my age and just going through this for the first time, with his life spread out before him, for God's sake, while I'm here with my life not spreading at all, because even if I stay clean I've only got, what, a dozen years left?

It's not just that it seemed, on the third visit, as you signed the clipboard, that you were a signatory to some insoluble time-sense, and that the duration of your visit would be a stasis of time that would forever play itself out in the revisiting of the situation from that particular point of time in relation to what happened later, and that would, in hindsight, seem marked, somehow, in relation to the way the hospital ward stood, even as you signed in, as a momentary, fleeting refuge from the wild torments of the outside world, the indelible real places—the old house on the river that had been empty since your brother's divorce, and the old art studio in the rehabilitated mill building where he had worked on his paintings, and the river itself, the shoreline down near the state park where he'd hiked with his son—that would when he thought back on them spark in him a need, a desire, to rehash his relationship with the chemicals that eased the pain they produced. It's not just that you're constantly embarrassed by or ashamed of the circularity of the story when you think of it. It's not just that no matter how hard you try to see his story in simple tragic terms, as an Aristotelian process, you also feel yourself spinning back into the cycle that might eventually devour him, losing touch with whatever cathartic elements might lie hidden within the structure of his story as it relates to your own, partly because you are still part of the story and it has yet to reach its terminus and therefore the overarching arc, its meaning, hasn't been reached yet—at least, so it seems.

It's not just that you went to the state park to walk one afternoon and found his boots near the edge of the palisade, the sheer drop-off to the shore of the river. It's not just that no matter how often you sort and pick through the story, alongside your parents and your sister and everyone else, you can't help but find yourself, against your better nature, feeling the big sway and spin of the cosmos—the dark eternal matter of the stars, which, however isotropic or evenly balanced, seem, when you think of him, to be moving in a circular pattern that reminds you that the nurse explained, each time, during each pre-visit orientation, that part of the healing process was to step off the merry-go-round and never step back on.

It's not just that so many of the organic compounds, landlocked by their restricting bonds, all those fuzzy quantum orbitals, tend toward formations that are elegantly circular. It's not just that he took his boots off and leaped from the palisade and lifted his hands and flew out over the river and then back and that he felt himself relinquished of his condition and totally free for a few seconds, with the water below him. It's not just that you imagined this as you sat in the car in the parking lot, after the third, maybe the fourth visit, with the smell of damp paper bag and steaming coffee and—between those smells—the bready bagel smell. It's not just that you only imagined the boots and then felt strange about the image, and remembered hiking back down the trail and along the railroad tracks to the road, stopping to stare at his house, now under new ownership, situated a quarter mile up the road from the stone quarry, the one you used in one of your stories, years back, when you were first beginning to locate the sober source of your own vision.

·

No, it's the fact that he never had a chance to fly and that you never really found those boots and that each time you visited him he seemed to be only slightly better. It's the fact that when you left him behind, speeding down the road past the old Rockland buildings, boarded up and unused now that most of the mad and crazy are outpatients, medicated, wandering the streets and the homeless shelters, you felt a keen elation. It's the fact that once again you were joyfully facing the harsh limitations of reality, admitting that it all had to be taken and turned into a story of some kind. Otherwise, it would just be one more expression of precise discontent. And expressions of discontent—you think in the car, sitting in front of your own house now—no matter how beautiful, never solve the riddle of the world, or bring the banality of sequential reality to a location of deeper grace.

MEMBERS

FABER

Become a Faber Member and discover the best in the arts and literature.

Sign up to the Faber Members programme and enjoy specially curated events, tailored discounts, and exclusive previews of our forthcoming publications from the best novelists, poets, playwrights, thinkers, musicians and artists.

ff

Join for free today at faber.co.uk/members